"Triple R"

by

Donald H. Jans

FADE IN:

EXT. JEFFERSON CITY - DAY

A highway BILLBOARD reads: WELCOME TO JEFFERSON CITY, HOME OF 3 FINE MC DONALD'S RESTAURANTS.

In the background, the DOME of the MISSOURI STATE CAPITOL BUILDING dominates a bedrock bluff in the rural capitol city.

EXT. CAPITOL BUILDING

A purple 1980 PURPLE MONZA SQUEALS around the capitol's circular driveway.

INT. PURPLE MONZA

ROCK MUSIC blares while bleached blond and blue eye-shadowed TRISHA TWEEDY (17) drives while dangerously powdering her nose in the rear view mirror.

TAMMY GIBSON (17), looking disturbingly similar, struggles to pull a heavy wool sweater with a LARGE J over her head without disturbing her shellacked hair or make-up.

The Monza skids to a stop in front of a FACULTY ONLY sign.

EXT. PURPLE MONZA

Tammy hops out of the car now dressed as a cheerleader. She freshens her mascara in the side mirror then reaches back in the car to retrieve something RED. She devilishly grins at Trisha before she spins around to enter a back door.

INT. GIRL'S LOCKER ROOM - DAY

In the shadows, young female HANDS anxiously fumble inside a small red and black gym bag on an anchored bench. Something WHITE is removed. The bag is quickly ZIPPED.

Leaning on the door jamb, MARILYN WEIR (49), dressed in a hot pink sleeveless shirt, black leggings and diamond studded cat eye reading glasses suspended on a gold chain, observes the person at the bag while smoking a thin cigarette. She jerks her head towards the din of the gymnasium.

                    MARILYN
               (Southern accent)
          You're fixin' to get caught.

Marilyn shoos the person away.

                    MARILYN (CONT'D)
          Not this way stupid.

The hands throw the WHITE and the PEN-LIKE OJBECT in a
swinging trash can.

Beautiful 17 year old natural blond, JUDY DAWSON, hurries
into the locker room carrying a stack of FLYERS. She is
dressed in perfectly fitting jeans and a flattering white t-
shirt.

                    MARILYN (CONT'D)
          Young lady you have 1500 people out there
          waiting on you.

                    JUDY
               (semi Valley girl)
          I totally tried, but I am so sure.

Judy tosses the enormous stack of "GO JAYBIRDS" flyers next
to the gym bag and begins to dress.

                    MARILYN
          Being a Jaybird cheerleader is an honor,
          not a duty.

Judy immodestly takes off her t-shirt and puts on her
cheerleader sweater. Marilyn leers at her body and grins.

                    JUDY
          Umm, could you like.

Judy rotates her hand for Marilyn to turn around. Marilyn
continues to stare. Judy frantically searches her gym bag.

                    JUDY (O.S.) (CONT'D)
          I know I had freshies in here.

Judy grabs the red polyester panties. She turns away from the
leering eye and puts them on underneath her skirt.

                    MARILYN
          Go, now girl.

Marilyn gently shoves Judy towards the roar. An evil grin
takes over Marilyn's face as she saunters towards the
gymnasium, playing with her eyeglass chain.

A SHADOW approaches the trash can, reaches its tanned
leathery HAND inside and retrieves a discarded SEAM RIPPER
and WHITE PANTIES WITH ORANGE CALIFORNIA POPPIES.

JONAS SKAGGS (45) holds the panties dressed in blue work
coveralls.

>   JONAS
>   Well what do we have here?

Jonas examines the items and takes a big SNIFF of the
underwear. He smiles, baring his rotten teeth and stuffs
them into his bib and resumes sweeping.

INT. HIGH SCHOOL GYMNASIUM

Welcome to a Jefferson City High School football game pep
rally in full swing.

100 young boosters, the JAYETTES, dressed in their Red and
Black 50's style uniforms, complete with saddle shoes, white
gloves, pleated skirts and black wool sweaters each with a
large red letter "J", move in poorly executed synchronization
waving their arms to their band's bad rendition of "Play that
Funky Music White Boy".

The stone cold crowd of prepsters, new-wavers, goat-ropers
and partiers remains unmoved.

Tammy and Trisha bask in the glow of their cheerleader status
in front of the ambivalent crowd. Tammy pops the elastic on
her panties to give the boys a thrill. Tammy then grabs a
CAN of hair spray from Trisha for her turn at solidifying her
perfectly feathered hair. Trisha COUGHS from the fumes.

Judy trudges up to her fellow cheerleaders holding her
flyers. BECKY (17) a perky Dorothy Hammill look-alike,
follows at her heels also carrying flyers.

>   TAMMY
>   (Trailer twang)
>   Hey Girl, where you been?

>   JUDY
>   Oh my God, there's like no way you two
>   finished.

>   TAMMY
>   Girl, you just throw them away when old
>   Marilyn's not looking.

Judy smiles and nods.

Becky throws her flyers down in disgust.

Tammy attempts a leg stretch to appear athletic as she looks
up at the stands towards CAROLYN (17), a chubbier version of
Tammy with worse make-up. She wears a 40's style man's hat
that reads PRESS in the hat band. Carolyn grins at Tammy
holding up her CAMERA.

Tammy spies her mother KAY GIBSON (40), looking in a small mirror picking her bleached blond beehive. A brass medallion that reads DIAMOND 1985 rests in her fire hazard.

> TRISHA
> Let's make some noise!

Tammy, Trisha, Judy and Becky clasp their hands above their heads in a line ready to cheer. Judy tries to care.

> CHEER
> We've got the power...to win. We're
> gonna tear 'em up...and then. We're
> gonna rip 'em up, tear 'em up, lay 'em on
> the line, cause it's power time a..gain.
> Jeff City power time...again!

All four kick their legs up in the air.

A CLOSE UP of Judy's red cover panties shows the seam at her crotch is ripping.

Tammy glances at Judy's crotch and nods to Carolyn in the stands taking photographs. Carolyn nods at Marilyn standing near the bleachers.

CAROLYN'S POV THROUGH THE LENS: Judy's skirt.

> CHEER (CONT'D)
> Jeff City is red hot! Jeff City is red
> hot! Jeff City is R-E-D Red! H-O-T
> Hot! Once we start we can't be
> stopped..woo!

> TAMMY
> Come on everybody! We can't hear you!

A Jayette moves a thick mat in front of the cheerleaders.

> CHEER
> Give me a J!

> CROWD
> J!

Tammy and Becky hunch over. Trisha climbs on their backs.

> CHEER
> Give me an E!

> CROWD
> E!

Judy prepares to climb the mini pyramid.

                    CHEER
          Give me an F!

                    CROWD
          F!

Judy climbs to the top of the girls and stands upright.

                    CHEER
          Give me another F!

                    CROWD
          F!

                    CHEER
          What does it spell?!

                    CROWD
          JEFF CITY!

Judy jumps off her perch and goes into her perfect spread eagle. (Suggest slow motion)

Carolyn guffaws and feverishly clicks her camera.

JUDY'S POV: Several boys hit their buddies and point at her crotch which has been completely bared.

4 preppily dressed girls point, laugh and sneer at Judy.

Judy's smile erases as she finally realizes her predicament and crumbles onto the mat, pulling her skirt down to her knees.

Tammy goes to Judy's aid but lets the crowd know she's in on the joke.

                    TAMMY
          What's the matter Judy?

                    JUDY
          Oh my God!

Judy holds her skirt down and scurries away to the maniacal LAUGHTER of the gymnasium.

INT. GIRL'S LOCKER ROOM - DAY

Judy weeps on the bench rocking back and forth wearing blue jeans underneath her skirt. Trisha and Tammy enter.

                    TRISHA
          Sweetie, what happened?

Trisha darts her eyes at Tammy. Tammy puts her hand on
Judy's shoulder.

                    JUDY
          These super cheap panties they gave us
          ripped during my eagle.

Judy holds up the panties.

                    TAMMY
          I'm sure nobody saw nothing.

Tammy looks at Trisha and smiles. Judy looks up, immediately
erasing their smiles.

                    JUDY
          I am so sure. It was a total gyno exam.

The crowd roars with commotion in the distance.

                    JUDY (CONT'D)
          I've got to get out of here.

                    TRISHA
          You coming to the river tonight?

                    JUDY
          Vagina girl is going to miss this one.

                    TAMMY
          We're here for you hon.

                    JUDY
          What-ever.

Judy grabs her bags and storms out of the locker room.

INT. JUDY'S KITCHEN - AFTERNOON

Judy's mom, JOAN(40) attractive and fit, dressed in khakis
and a white blouse, stirs a pot of spaghetti sauce in her
vintage sunny kitchen. Judy storms in the door.

                    JOAN
          Hi Judy! How was your day sweetie?

                    JUDY
               (in French)
          Fucking shitty.

                    JOAN
          That's nice you're practicing your French
          honey.

Joan looks up, noticing her sadness.

                    JOAN (CONT'D)
          Bet it's nothing your favorite spaghetti
          sauce won't fix.

Joan presents a wooden spoon to Judy.

                    JUDY
          I can't eat.

                    JOAN
          But honey, you're so thin.

                    JUDY
          Not this again.

                    JOAN
          Want to tell me about it?

                    JUDY
          Too embarrassing.

Judy takes the spoon and dips it in the sauce for a taste.

                    JOAN
          Is it about a boy? I was 16 once you
          know.

                    JUDY
          I'm 17, and if it were only that easy.
          There's so many horny goat ropers and
          bitches in this town. Why the hell did
          we have to move here!

                    JOAN
          Language honey. You know this job was a
          big promotion for your father. It would
          break his heart to know you hate it so
          much here.

                    JUDY
          Everything doesn't have to be like so
          Stepford perfect mom. We're not in
          California anymore, in case you didn't
          notice.

Judy's brother Scott waltzes in the door. SCOTT DAWSON is a
15 year old handsome gangly pre-stud.

                    SCOTT
          Hi mom. Hey Jude.

                    JOAN
          Hi Honey!

                    SCOTT
          Hey Jude is it true?

Scott takes his two fingers and bounces them up in the air
and spreads them.

                    JUDY
          Yup.

                    SCOTT
          No way, nice.

Scott can't erase his smile. Joan is oblivious, stirring her
spaghetti. Judy grabs her bag and heads to her room.

Scott dips his finger into the bubbling spaghetti and quickly
licks it.

                    SCOTT (CONT'D)
          Ow!

Joan regains control of her spaghetti pot.

                    JOAN
          Put it in a bowl, honey.

INT. JUDY'S BEDROOM - AFTERNOON

Judy lays on her flowery bedspread talking sadly on the
phone.

                    JUDY
          Omigod Barb, it was like "Carrie".
          Everything was in slow motion except no
          one was throwing tampons at me.

EXT. BEACH DECK - PACIFIC PALISADES- DAY

BARB is a 17-year-old hot beach muffin clad in a skimpy
bikini, complete with world-class breasts.

Barb sits on her beach deck sunning herself sipping an iced
tea, giggling.

                    BARB
               (full valley girl)
          So freaky. You're still trimmed up
          there, right?

INTERCUT AS NEEDED

                    JUDY
          God Barb, yes. You should see the super
          hairy bushes on some of these girls in
          gym class. It's like seriously braidable.

Judy gets up, blocking our view, and lifts up her skirt to
the full length mirror and sits down contented.

                    BARB
          Then what are you worrying about? Dates
          will be rolling in.

                    JUDY
          I don't even have any girlfriends.

                    BARB
          Well if it makes you feel any better, it
          sucks here without you. At least you're
          on a total adventure.

                    JUDY
          I'm so glad you're enjoying it.

                    BARB
          Oh, please, please, please tell me about
          the sorority again. You've got to do it!

                    JUDY
          Everyone already got their invites.

                    BARB
          I'm sorry sweetie. How could they not
          want the hottest girl ever?

                    JUDY
          I'm definitely "Ok" with it.

Judy sighs and touches her bedspread.

                    BARB
          Chin up babe. You'll be back in sunny
          Cal before you know it.

                    JUDY
          Thanks for being a friend Barb.

                    BARB
          Call Quarterback cutie right now.

                    JUDY
               (mockingly)
          I'm sure he's at the big "bonfire".

Judy lays back on her bed trying to mask her disappointment and puts a pillow over her crotch.

EXT. BONFIRE - EVENING

Throngs of students ring a bonfire holding keg cups, smoking, chewing tobacco and talking. A small line forms at the keg.

Trisha and Tammy, dressed in preppy wool monogrammed sweaters, khaki skirts and gold add-a-bead necklaces, stand near MITCH (17), ultimate stud, and two letterman, RYAN and SEAN all quaffing beers.

                    MITCH
          Where's Judy?

Trisha grins.

                    TRISHA
          You heard about her little incident
          didn't you?

Mitch and his letterman laugh and hit each other. Tammy gets jealous and cozies up to Mitch.

                    TAMMY
          What do you need her for when you've got
          me?

Tammy bats her blue-eye shadowed eyes and swoons toward Mitch giving him a big wet kiss on the lips. He wipes it off. Tammy turns him away from the fire.

Sean hits Ryan as they look at Mitch.

                    MITCH
          I'll catch you fellers later.

Mitch slaps a high five to his gang as he leaves with Tammy. Trisha is left alone with Ryan and Sean.

                    TRISHA
          Guess it's just me and ya'all.

Trisha shrugs as Ryan and Sean surround her.

                                        SMASH TO:

INT. WHITE CHEVY VAN - EVENING

In the shadows, Trisha is fully clothed holding a POLAROID camera. Sean and Ryan are completely naked covering their crotches.

                    TRISHA
          Ok, grab his thingie.

Ryan reaches a hand out toward Sean. Sean bats it away.

                    SEAN
          Get off it dude. Come on Trisha. We've
          done enough...you said.

                    RYAN
          What's the big deal? Remember Camp
          Ozark?

Sean hits Ryan hard in the shoulder. Ryan rubs his shoulder.

                    TRISHA
          Momma just needs a little insurance
          policy that you boys are gonna keep your
          traps shut.

                    SEAN
          You wanna be Homecoming Queen or not?

                    TRISHA
          But do you want "this" or not?

Trisha runs her hand the length of her body.

Sean grabs towards Ryan's crotch and pains a smile for the
camera. CLICK, WHIRRRRRR.

                    TRISHA (CONT'D)
          Excellent.

Trisha takes her gum out, sticks it to the roof of the van
and eagerly disrobes.

MOMENTS LATER:

                    TRISHA (CONT'D)
          God damn it! You Asshole!

Trisha rolls out of her position.

                    TRISHA (CONT'D)
          I said none of that. You can use Sean's.

                    RYAN
          Sorry. Thought it might be a little
          tighter.

Dull LAUGHTER rumbles from Sean and Ryan.

                    TRISHA
          Fuck you guys.

Trisha angrily finds her clothes.

                    TRISHA (CONT'D)
          You boys don't know how to treat a real
          woman.

                    SEAN
          Whadya mean?

                    TRISHA
          You don't have any class. These are
          class.

Trisha calms down and moves her head back to show her
earrings as Sean fondles her ear.

                    SEAN
          Cool, those are shiny.

Sean moves her head back and forth to make them glisten in
the street light.

                    SEAN (CONT'D)
          Where'd you get 'em?

Sean moves her head back and forth a little more as Trisha
begins to smile. Sean inches her head closer to his crotch.
She punches Sean away.

                    TRISHA
          Never mind.

A spotlight flashes on the van.

                    SEAN
          Fuck! It's Skippie.

All frantically attempt to put their clothes on. Trisha
takes cover underneath a blanket. The flashlight catches
Sean's face.

SKIP is a sturdy 45 year old cop.

                    SKIP
          Good game Sean.

Skip shines the FLASHLIGHT on shirtless Ryan. The boys look
at each other.

                         SKIP (CONT'D)
              I don't think so. Who else you got in
              there?

Trisha's bare ankle pokes out from underneath the blanket
near Sean's butt.

                         SKIP (CONT'D)
              Come on outta there.

Trisha pokes her head up from the blanket, eyes squinting
from the direct flashlight.

                         TRISHA
              Please don't tell momma Marilyn.

The boys look puzzled at Trisha who quickly puts on her
clothes.

                         SKIP
              Young lady. I'd like a word with you.

Skip and Trisha walk towards the trees as she continues
tucking her shirt.

                         SEAN
              Ole Skippy's probably gonna try to get a
              piece of her too.

Sean and Ryan continue to dress as they watch Skip who firmly
points his finger at Trisha who covers her face and throws
her hands down in desperation. Skip and Trisha walk back to
the boys van.

                         SKIP
              You boys take her home right away, ya
              hear?

                         SEAN
              We were gonna stop by Dairy Queen for a
              Soft Serve.

                         SKIP
              I think Trisha had enough cream for one
              night.

The boys chuckle. Trisha fumes looking out the window with
her arms crossed.

                         SEAN
              Yessir. We'll take her straight away.

The boys and Trisha start to drive away.

                    RYAN
          You ain't doing nothing with him are you?

                    TRISHA
          You're sick. And you best be keeping
          your mouths shut.

Trisha holds the POLAROID. Sean grabs for it. Trisha stuffs
it in her bra.

                    SEAN
          This is bullshit, I didn't even bust a
          nut.

Sean's face goes blank, and then excited.

                    SEAN (CONT'D)
          Fuck yeah! Love this song.

Sean cranks his Pioneer stereo. Suggest "Girls Got Rhythm"
AC/DC

Trisha plugs her ears and shakes her head.

INT. JUDY'S BEDROOM - MORNING

Judy shakes her head having just brushed her hair at the
mirror. Scott knocks and enters.

                    SCOTT
          So, you going to school today?

Scott jumps up and attempts a spread eagle trying to touch
his toes.

                    JUDY
          You've got to point your toes more.

Judy throws the ripped red cover panties in the wastebasket
and heads out of her room.

Scott looks to see that she has gone; retrieves her red
panties from the wastebasket; stuffs them in his backpack and
exits the room.

INT. JUDY'S KITCHEN - MORNING

Joan scrambles eggs and sausage while Judy fills her orange
juice glass.

                    JOAN
          Honey, you are going to eat something.

                         JUDY
          Mom, you're like a total greasy Betty
          Crocker now. What happened to fruit and
          cereal?

                         JOAN
          Mrs. Gibson dropped off some fresh
          sausage.

                         JUDY
          Then you eat it.

                         JOAN
          It was a very nice gesture.

                         JUDY
          It probably has parts of her missing
          husband in it.

Scott walks in and kisses his mother and fixes himself a
plate. Joan puts her hands on her hips.

                         JOAN
          Young lady, she pulled some pretty big
          strings to get you into cheerleading.

                         JUDY
          And that's been super! Thank God I'm
          almost done. California here I come. I
          totally feel for you, Scotty.

Judy's father, KIRK,(40) handsome and fit, walks in behind
Judy.

                         KIRK
               (affected Southern drawl)
          Morning ya'all.

Kirk kisses Judy.

                         JUDY
          You're scaring me dad.

                         KIRK
               (normal voice)
          Pumpkin, you just have to give this place
          a chance and you'll be Miss Popularity
          again before you know it.

Judy pleads on his arm.

                         JUDY
              Dad! This is like a bad dream. We are
              living in the state capitol that no one
              has ever heard of.

                         KIRK
              Well,once I put my dues in designing
              their sewer system, I can write my ticket
              anywhere.

                         JUDY
              The things I do for you.

Judy kisses her dad, shakes her head and grabs a banana.

                         JUDY (CONT'D)
              Off to another fun filled day of culture
              and mind expansion.

Judy trounces out the door while her dad smiles.

INT. HALLWAY- JEFFERSON CITY HIGH SCHOOL - MORNING

Judy approaches her locker. She notices a PICTURE stuck to
the front. A gaggle of girls stand nearby waiting for her
reaction. It is stuck with super glue.

CLOSE UP: A black and white PICTURE of Judy during her spread
eagle. A caption over the crotch reads: Over 40 billion
served.

Judy attempts to pull it off. Scott approaches carrying a
stack of identical torn up pictures.

                         SCOTT
              Hey, I think I got most of them.

                         JUDY
              Thanks.

Judy throws the pictures in her locker.

Becky approaches with a sneer and hands Judy a MEMO.

                         BECKY
              Mrs. Weir wants to see you right away.

Judy rolls her eyes and slams her locker.

EXT. MARILYN WEIR'S OFFICE

Judy looks through a large glass window that reads MARILYN
WEIR COUNSELOR. A disheveled Trisha sits across from
Marilyn.

Marilyn sees Judy peering in and abruptly pulls the shade to her window.

Judy shakes her head and turns around pulling her binder to her chest.

2 preppily dressed girls walk by Judy, point and snicker.

Judy shoots a big fake smile at them.

>   JUDY
>   Ya'all have a good day now, ya hear?

Trisha storms out of Marilyn's office and bumps into Judy.

>   TRISHA
>   She is such a bitch.

>   JUDY
>   Great.

Trisha continues away.

Judy holds her white office memo and looks at it.

Judy walks into Marilyn's office.

INT. MARILYN WEIR'S OFFICE

>   MARILYN
>   Have a seat Judy.

Judy complies.

>   MARILYN (CONT'D)
>   It seems you weren't wearing any
>   underwear underneath your cheerleader
>   skirt. What kind of school do you think
>   this is?

>   JUDY
>   You tell me.

The phone RINGS. Marilyn picks it up.

>   MARILYN
>   Well, hello there.

She covers the phone.

>   MARILYN (CONT'D)
>   This is private. Wait outside.

She nods toward the door, Judy complies. Marilyn closes the door behind Judy.

INT. CAPITOL BUILDING OFFICE - DAY

CHET, a 50 year old grey haired chubby tanned huckster, practices putting in his beautiful wood paneled office as he talks on the speaker phone.

                    CHET
          Marilyn, you little vixen. How's my #1
          girl doing.

INTERCUT AS NEEDED

                    MARILYN
          Doing great Chet. Just got your recent
          donation, thank you very much.

Chet picks up a PHOTOGRAPH of Judy doing her spread eagle and phwacks his fingers against it.

                    CHET
          How come this new cheerleader girl ain't
          a Triple R girl.

                    MARILYN
          We only got her on the squad so we'd look
          good at away games. We're just having a
          little fun with her.

                    CHET
          Well I want Miss Spread Eagle.

                    MARILYN
          Chet, it's your rule about no out-a-
          towners.

                    CHET
          Then I can break it.

                    MARILYN
          But--

                    CHET
          No buts. I take care of my girls. Did
          Trisha show you those diamond I got her?

                    MARILYN
          She had them on this morning, proud as a
          peacock.

                    CHET
          That's right.

Chet putts, the ball rolls in the hole.

> MARILYN
> Which is why I'm calling. I want you to
> hear this from me first instead of Skip.

> CHET
> Who needs a ticket taken care of this
> time?

> MARILYN
> Seems your favorite little Trisha was
> caught celebrating with the football team
> in a little gang bang down near Frog
> Hollow.

> CHET
> That little bitch!

Chet putts.

> CHET (CONT'D)
> She knows the rules.

The ball misses the hole.

> CHET (CONT'D)
> I don't need to be getting a drippy dick
> from one of those punks.

Chet BANGS the side of his desk with his club.

> MARILYN
> Now Chet, don't get in a lather. I've
> talked to her and she won't do it again.

> CHET
> I want her checked out by Doc Gardner.

> MARILYN
> Consider it done.

> CHET
> I saw that new Buick Regal you've been
> riding in, thank you very much.

> MARILYN
> Just my 20% Chet, not a penny more.

> CHET
> You sure ain't cheap. But you never was
> even when we was kids taking my red hots
> for a peek at your boo-boo.

                    MARILYN
          And who's been bringing you and your boys
          the best for 30 years.

                    CHET
          That's why you're my #1 girl. So don't
          let me down on Miss Eagle.

                    MARIL
          This ol' girl has a couple more tricks up
          her sleeve.

                    CHET
          Atta girl.

Chet putts again and makes it.

Marilyn hangs up, hops up and opens the door. Her demeanor
changes to sickeningly sweet. She motions Judy to sit down.

Mrs. Weir folds her hands and clears her throat.

                    MARILYN
          Sweetie, I don't think you are hanging
          out with the right crowd.

                    JUDY
          Um, I don't have a crowd.

                    MARILYN
          How would you like to finally be popular?

                    JUDY
               (sarcastically)
          You mean it?

The sarcasm shoots right over Marilyn's head as she pulls out
a white RRR INVITATION.

                    MARILYN
          Normally this is reserved for Jefferson
          City Royalty. But for you, I think we
          could make an exception.

Mrs. Weir looks at her jewelry.

                    JUDY
          Thanks, but no thanks.

Marilyn tries to maintain her anger.

                    MARILYN
          It's been a wonderful tradition for over
          60 years here in Jefferson City. I was a
          Triple R girl myself.

                    JUDY
          But they totally exclude people. What
          about Lori Brown? She's a total sweet
          heart, and she actually wants to be in
          it.

                    MARILYN
          Well, Lori doesn't quite have what it
          takes.

                    JUDY
          So what does it take?

                    MARILYN
          A special girl like you.

She extends her palm to Judy. Judy stares at her blank-
faced.

                    JUDY
          Thanks anyway.

                    MARILYN
          You will be a member!

Judy looks alarmed. Mrs. Weir backs down and clears her
throat.

                    MARILYN (CONT'D)
          What I mean is, I think you have the will
          to be a member.

                    JUDY
          Is that what this meeting is about?

Judy gets up to exit.

                    MARILYN
          A lot of privileges come with being a
          Triple R girl. You can make your life a
          lot easier...or difficult.

Marilyn pulls out one of the captioned PICTURES of Judy in
her spread eagle and places it on a stack of papers.

                    JUDY
          I'll take my chances.

Judy grumbles out of the office.

INT. SCOTT'S BEDROOM - AFTERNOON

Scott and Billy Sundermeyer analyze Judy's red polyester
cheerleading panties underneath a MAGNIFYING GLASS.

BILLY SUNDERMEYER (15) is a bespectacled super nerd.

> BILLY
> According to my hypotheses, these seem to
> have been ripped prior to the "spread
> eagle incident" with what appears to be a
> sharp instrument. Here look.

Scott takes the magnifying glass and panties.

> SCOTT
> Whoa...I see it. I knew something
> smelled fishy.

> BILLY
> Does it?

Billy takes the panties back and puts them to his nose.
Scott grabs them back and slams them on the table.

> BILLY (CONT'D)
> According to my crime magazine, every
> crime must have a motive, and of course a
> perpetrator.

> SCOTT
> No one can know we're doing this.

> BILLY
> Yes sir, top secret.

Scott rolls his eyes.

Billy stuffs the panties in his pocket.

> SCOTT
> I'll keep those.

Billy looks embarrassed.

> BILLY
> At 1700 hours.

> SCOTT
> Gotcha.

Billy leaves. Scott shakes his head and hides the panties.

                    SCOTT (CONT'D)
          What a perv.

Scott turns on the TV and plays Atari's "Breakout". Judy
lightly knocks and enters.

                    JUDY
          So, you hanging out with Einstein these
          days?

                    SCOTT
          The friend pool is kind of limited.

Judy sits on the bed.

                    JUDY
          I hear ya. Just a little while longer.

                    SCOTT
          It's gonna totally suck when you
          graduate.

Judy tussles his hair.

                    JUDY
          You'll just have to come visit big sister
          at college.

                    SCOTT
          Who's going to look out for you?

                    JUDY
          I look out for you.

Judy squeezes Scott's bicep, playfully squeezes and then
tickles him.

INT. JUDY'S KITCHEN - EVENING

Judy, Scott, Kirk and Joan laugh and enjoy a candlelit steak
dinner.

Scott gets up to leave.

                    SCOTT
          My show's on.

                    JOAN
          Say "excuse me".

Scott gives his mom's hairdo a one handed claw massage and
says nothing as he walks out.

Judy looks at her watch and starts to get up.

                    JOAN (CONT'D)
          Your dad and I would like to talk to you.

                    JUDY
          Oh my God Mrs. Carpenter, I ate
          everything.

Judy displays her clean plate.

                    JOAN
          We got a call from Mrs. Weir today.

Judy grows a snotty look but is somewhat fearful.

                    JUDY
          About what?

                    JOAN
          Honey, I know you've had problems fitting
          in, and this Triple R sounds like the
          perfect answer.

                    JUDY
          Mom.

                    JOAN
          Do you think you're better than the other
          girls? Is that it?

                    JUDY
          Yeah, that's exactly it mom.

                    JOAN
          Is it because you don't like the way they
          dress?

Judy closes her eyes. She can't believe how stupid her
mother is being.

                    KIRK
          Judy, tell you what. You try it for 2
          months and I'll get you a plane ticket to
          go see Barb.

                    JOAN
          It sounds like a great bunch of gals.

                    KIRK
          If you don't like it you can quit!

                    JUDY
          Why don't you guys do it.

Judy longs after a family BEACH PICTURE resting on the
banquet.

                    JUDY (CONT'D)
          They'll make me feather my hair.

                    JOAN
          I think it looks kind of cute.

                    JUDY
          Mom, you also think little pigs are cute.

Kirk smiles as Judy throws down her napkin and leaves the
room.

                    KIRK
          Think about it honey.

                    JOAN
          Well they are, those little noses.

Joan upturns her nose with a finger. Kirk leans over to kiss
her, completely in love.

INT. JUDY'S FAMILY ROOM - EVENING

Scott hogs the leather couch. Judy enters the room and plops
down in the matching chair, her legs over the arm. "Hart to
Hart" plays in the background.

                    JUDY
          Dude, Joan and Kirk are fully
          blackmailing me about joining Triple R.

                    SCOTT
          How high have you driven the price?

                    JUDY
          The initial offer was a plane ticket to
          Barb.

                    SCOTT
          No way! I'll join.

Scott sits up.

                    JUDY
          Doesn't matter, I'm not doing it anyway.

                    SCOTT
          Judy.(Pause) Are you fucking stupid?!

Scott stands up. Judy is wide-eyed.

                    SCOTT (CONT'D)
          Who do you think is behind all this?

Judy shrugs.

                    SCOTT (CONT'D)
          Ok. Let me recap. First of all.

SERIES OF SHOTS:

INT. BIOLOGY CLASSROOM

Judy opens her purse revealing a dead baby pig. Several
people stand around waiting for her reaction.

                    SCOTT (O.S.)
          A fetal pig walks into your purse.

INT. CLASSROOM

Judy's hair is stuck to the back of her chair. Lori comes to
her rescue, carefully cutting it away.

                    SCOTT (O.S.)
          Someone glues your hair to a chair.

                    JUDY (O.S.)
          They were total split ends anyway.

EXT. JUDY'S HOUSE - EVENING

A purple Monza spins circles in the front lawn.

                    SCOTT (O.S.)
          Then, my fine meticulous yard work on the
          riding lawn mower is destroyed.

INT. FAMILY ROOM

                    SCOTT
          And let's not forget the latest "pies de
          la resistance".

Scott jumps up from the arm of the couch and touches his
toes.

                    JUDY
          You're getting better at that.

                    SCOTT
          Thanks, I've been practicing.

Scott sits next to Judy.

                    SCOTT (CONT'D)
          It's better to have your enemies in front
          of you than behind you.

                    JUDY
          Where'd you get so smart?

                    SCOTT
          Then you can find out what's so "secret"
          about it.

Judy sits in silence, thinking.

                    SCOTT (CONT'D)
          And, once you've been in it, you're
          golden, and you can assist me on my quest
          for Mrs. Dawson.

                    JUDY
          The only thing golden is going to be my
          ass on Newport Beach. If you played
          football, you'd be golden too.

                    SCOTT
          But I am the "man" without football.

Scott jumps up and spreads his arms and flexes.

                    SCOTT (CONT'D)
          I am the enforcer.

Scott jumps on Judy and tickles her as she YELPS and laughs.

INT. TRISHA'S BASEMENT - EVENING

In a dark, green shag carpeted basement, Trisha, Tammy, Becky
and Carolyn sit on pillows around an 8 foot long coffee table
lit by tea candles. Becky chats with Carolyn.

                    BECKY
          ...we got it so good here, my cousin in
          Arkansas said the Governor puts cigar
          tubes--

                    TRISHA
          --This meeting will now come to order.

Becky and Carolyn continue to finish their conversation.

                    TAMMY
          Silence! Carolyn, Becky, that's another
          50 cent fine.

Trisha passes a yellow PIGGY BANK with RRR painted in Blue.

Carolyn and Becky begrudgingly oblige with their coins,
CLINK, CLINK.

>   TRISHA
>   Now, a few things to talk about...the new
>   pledges.

Trisha points to Tammy.

>   TRISHA (CONT'D)
>   Tammy has compiled a list of blackballs
>   and potentials.

Tammy hands Trisha a stack of member's BIOS with their
pictures.

>   TRISHA (CONT'D)
>   First, and most fun, the blackballs.

Trisha puts the bios in front of her. She pulls out one of a
frumpy girl with a curly afro and glasses.

Trisha looks around excitedly.

>   TRISHA (CONT'D)
>   Can we all just say it!

>   GROUP (IN UNISON)
>   Ewwwwwwwww!

>   TRISHA
>   Perms are so out and feathered is in.
>   Where has she been?

Trisha proudly touches her hairsprayed flank of blond hair,
confident she's on the cutting edge.

>   TRISHA (CONT'D)
>   Out!

Trisha tosses the bio aside.

>   TRISHA (CONT'D)
>   Lori Brown!

Trisha holds the bio showing a girl in coke bottle glasses,
pigtails and acne.

>   TRISHA (CONT'D)
>   Mmmmmm....makes me hungry for pizza!
>   Out! She needs to oxycute those suckers.

She tosses it aside.

                    BECKY
          How did Miss California bitch like her
          little surprise?

                    TAMMY
          A few more weeks and we'll have her
          screaming down the halls naked.

Trisha jumps up and whispers in Tammy's ear.

                    TAMMY (CONT'D)
          But, maybe we should give her another
          chance.

                    CAROLYN
          What for? She thinks she's such hot shit.

                    TAMMY
          We're in charge Carolyn. I want you all
          to be extra nice, sincere and sweet.
          Anything else?

                    TRISHA
          Super secret, but Skip busted me with
          french fry dick and Sean in his van last
          night.

                    TAMMY
          You didn't tell him about Mitch did you?

                    TRISHA
          No way sister. We've got our reputations
          and virginity to uphold.

                    TAMMY
          Thank you. Remember girls "once your
          reputation is lost, it's lost forever,
          just like your virginity."

Tammy nods at Carolyn to continue.

                    CAROLYN
                (emotionless)
          To save your soul, have him poke the
          other hole.

Tammy nods at Becky.

                    BECKY
          To save your chastity, your pooper is
          where it has-to-be.

                    TAMMY
          That's right.

                    BECKY
                (to Carolyn)
            Yours rhymes better.

Tammy stares for silence.

                    TRISHA
            Did y'all see what Chet gave me?

Trisha shows her new earrings to Becky and Carolyn.

                    BECKY
            Nice work.

                    CAROLYN
            How come you get Chet and I get that
            meanie from Sedalia?

Carolyn shows a black bruise on her inner arm.

                    CAROLYN (CONT'D)
            He's so rough. I'm not doing it anymore.

                    TAMMY
            You will do as you are told. Trisha and
            I sure as hell aren't doing it.

                    TRISHA
            You want a free ride to State or not?

                    CAROLYN
            I guess, but--

                    TAMMY
            Who you guys taking to Homecoming?

Becky and Carolyn erupt in chatter. Trisha smiles like the
cat who swallowed the canary.

INT. HALLWAY JEFFERSON CITY HIGH SCHOOL - MORNING

A boy tickles a girl from behind standing in a hallway lined
with windows. Trisha and Judy stand nearby. Jonas mops in
the background observing the girls.

                    TRISHA
            I'm so glad you changed your mind.

Trisha hands Judy an envelope.

                    TRISHA (CONT'D)
         Here's an invitation to our Rush party.
         The theme is "Diaper Days".

                    JUDY
         Kinda kinky isn't it?

                    TRISHA
         You have to dress like a baby, silly.

                    JUDY
         Oh.

                    TRISHA
         Also, who's your date to homecoming?
         All pledges dates must be pre-approved.

                    JUDY
         Uhhh...Lori Brown.

Trisha tightens her lips.

                    TRISHA
         Pretending you're nice is good, so I
         suppose that's ok, but you don't want
         people thinking you're a lezzie.

Judy nods unable to speak, Trisha turns and walks away. Judy
shakes her head and looks at the invitation.

Judy folds the envelope and smushes it in her backpack.

Becky walks past Judy with a huge fake smile.

                    BECKY
         Hi Judy!

                    JUDY
         Hi.

Judy waves in bemusement.

EXT. STUDENT PARKING LOT

Judy walks with acne-ridden super geek LORI BROWN (17).

                    LORI
         I've never been to a dance. Aren't you
         supposed to go with a boy?

                    JUDY
         You can go with whoever you want.

MR. SONTAG (25), dressed like Mr. Rogers, walks to his
sparkle blue Chevette past Judy and Lori.

                    MR. SONTAG
          Afternoon ladies.

                    JUDY
          Hi Mr. Sontag.

                    MR. SONTAG
          Don't forget about the quiz tomorrow.

                    JUDY
          How could I?

Judy pats her large Biology book.

A large lift-kitted truck roars by.

                    MALE VOICE (O.S.)
          Faggot! Woo!

Judy looks at Mr. Sontag's pained face. She recognizes the
back of Sean and Ryan's head in the crowded cab wearing
cowboy hats.

                    MR. SONTAG
          That's ok.

                    JUDY
          No it's not.

                    MR. SONTAG
          So we'll see you tomorrow.

                    JUDY
          Count on it.

Mr. Sontag drives off in his Chevette. Judy checks off one
of a hundred BOXES with a pen on her notebook.

                    JUDY (CONT'D)
          173 days left.

                    LORI
          What?

                    JUDY
          Nothing.

                    LORI
          Mr. Sontag is cute.

                    JUDY
          Do you want to study later?

                    LORI
          That'd be fun.

                    JUDY
          The cheat and brown nose method isn't
          going to work in his class.

They get into Judy's green LTD wood paneled station wagon.

INT. PURPLE MONZA - AFTERNOON

Trisha and Tammy smoke Virginia Slims while driving out of
the school parking lot. They observe Judy and Lori getting
into the station wagon.

                    TRISHA
          I can't believe she's making us take her.
          Lori is going to totally ruin our image.

                    TAMMY
          It's going to be the highest point in her
          zit-popping life. OH SHIT! I forgot my
          book.

                    TRISHA
          When'd you start doing homework? I ain't
          got time to wait for you girl.

                    TAMMY
          Just drop me off. I'll get a ride with
          somebody.

                    TRISHA
          Or on somebody.

Tammy slams the car door on smirking Trisha.

INT. GIRL'S LOCKER ROOM - AFTERNOON

Tammy hides in the shadows watching Billy and Scott talking
with Jonas. Scott holds the red polyester panties. Jonas
shakes his head and points out the door. Billy and Scott
exit. Tammy approaches Jonas.

                    TAMMY
          What did those twerps want?

                    JONAS
          Probably looking for these?

Jonas pulls out Judy's cotton panties from his bib and sniffs them. Tammy lunges for them as Jonas evades her.

                    TAMMY
          Where'd you get those?

                    JONAS
          Right over there. Just where you left
          them.

                    TAMMY
          Goddamn you. What did you tell them?

                    JONAS
          Nothing. Yet. You might think I'm some
          big stupid but I've been around since
          your momma thought she was fancy pants
          too.

                    TAMMY
          What do you want?

                    JONAS
          Now we're talking.

Jonas rubs his hands together.

                    JONAS (CONT'D)
          Just a little bit of that loving you've
          been sharing around.

                    TAMMY
          And if not?

                    JONAS
          I know a couple young detectives who'd be
          mighty interested in these.

Jonas snickers and dangles the seam ripper next to the panties, stuffing them away.

                    TAMMY
          Ok, but I get those. You better not tell
          no one.

Tammy crosses her arms and glares at him.

                    JONAS
          I'd take real good care of you.

Jonas puts his arms around her. She shrugs it off.

                    TAMMY
          But I'm in charge.

Tammy waggles her finger at him.

                    JONAS
        Whatever you say my lady.

Jonas leads Tammy to a second story walkway which surrounds
the indoor pool.

                    JONAS (CONT'D)
        This looks as good a place as any.

Tammy takes her gum out and gets on her knees. Jonas undoes
his overalls with his back turned.

                    TAMMY
        Ewwwwww. What's that skin there?

                    JONAS
        It's European.

Tammy looks sternly at Jonas and shakes her finger again.

                    TAMMY
        You are NOT peeing on me.

Tammy plugs her nose and goes in.

Time passes.

Jonas's face writhes in joy. Tammy's eyes show her
impatience and annoyance. Jonas leans against a rusted and
stressed RAILING. The railing breaks free. Jonas loses his
balance and grabs on to Tammy's hair.

                    TAMMY (CONT'D)
        Get your grimy hands offa my hair!

Tammy pushes him backwards unaware of the broken railing.
Jonas falls backwards and lands with a bone cracking thud.

Tammy looks down and observes his unnatural position and his
open EYES. She pops her gum back in her mouth.

                    TAMMY (CONT'D)
        Awwww shit!

Tammy runs down the stairs while vigorously wiping her mouth
and tongue with her shirt. She grabs the seam ripper and
panties from his bib.

                    TAMMY (CONT'D)
        See what you did!

She looks around and scurries away.

INT. JUDY'S KITCHEN - EVENING

Scott and Judy haphazardly do the dishes.

>   JUDY
>   No, you're cleaning that. I did all the
>   other stuff.

Judy shoves a dirty baked-on glass casserole dish towards
Scott.

>   SCOTT
>   No way. That'll take an hour.

Judy sprays Scott with the sink sprayer.

>   JUDY
>   Your hour.

>   SCOTT
>   Now you're gonna get it.

Scott opens the freezer and grabs an ICE CREAM CONTAINER. He
opens it and licks the entire surface.

>   JUDY
>   I've already hidden all the pop-tarts and
>   the frosted animal cookies.

Scott stops licking.

>   JOAN (O.S.)
>   Judy, your friend Lori is here.

>   JUDY
>   (super sweet)
>   Ok Mother, coming.

Judy makes an "ah-hah" face at Scott.

>   JOAN (O.S.)
>   Are you two ready for inspection?

>   SCOTT
>   Yes mother.

Scott throws the casserole dish in the trash and cinches the
bag.

Joan walks in the kitchen.

                    SCOTT (CONT'D)
          Just taking out the garbage mother.

                    JOAN
          You're so helpful honey. Judy finish up
          the counter top.

Joan caresses Scott's face as she walks out.

Judy stares in disgust at Scott's innocent smile.

                    JUDY
          You little shit.

Scott heads out the door. Judy throws a mildewed sponge.

                    JUDY (CONT'D)
          Incoming.

Scott spins around. The sponge hits him square in the face
with brilliant aim.

                    SCOTT
          Oooh.

Judy walks into the foyer.

INT. JUDY'S FOYER - EVENING

Lori stands smiling with her books over her chest.

                    JUDY
          Come on back.

                    LORI
          Nice house.

                    JUDY
          Thanks.

INT. JUDY'S BEDROOM

Books and papers litter the bed around Judy and Lori. Both
ponder into their books.

                    LORI
          This is so romantic. This robin, when it
          mates. It will fall in embrace towards
          the ground until it has finished.

                    JUDY
          Wonder what happens if Mr. Bird can't get
          off?

Judy smacks her hands together. Lori's face turns red.

                    LORI
          Those poor birds.

                    JUDY
          Well at least they would die having fun.

                    LORI
          I wouldn't know. No guys look at me.

Judy closes her book.

                    JUDY
          If you want, I could help you with a few
          beauty tricks.

                    LORI
          Could you?

Judy scoots over to Lori as she closes her book. Judy pulls
Lori's hair away from her face as they both gaze towards the
door mirror.

                    JUDY
          First of all, these.

Judy removes Lori's large plastic coke-bottle glasses and
reveals Lori's pretty face.

                    JUDY (CONT'D)
          Ever thought about contacts?

                    LORI
          I have them. They just take so long to
          put in.

                    JUDY
          They're a snap once you get used to them.
          And what about face cleanser.

                    LORI
          Oh I know.

Lori touches her blemished face.

                    LORI (CONT'D)
          The doctor says I'm allergic to
          chocolate.

                    JUDY
          And.

                    LORI
          I love chocolate!

                    JUDY
          So don't eat it.

                    LORI
          I can't give up chocolate!

                    JUDY
          You want a cute boyfriend or not?

                    LORI
          Cute boyfriend.

                    JUDY
          Ok then.

Some time later.

INT. JUDY'S BATHROOM - EVENING

Judy and Lori stand facing the mirror. Lori's hair covers
her face as Judy trims carefully with scissors, zeroing in on
a stray hair.

                    JUDY
          Alfalfa be gone.

Lori raises her head slowly. She looks spectacular dressed
in a sexy number of Judy's, complete with new makeup. Judy
dusts the finishing touches of makeup on Lori.

                    JUDY (CONT'D)
          You are a serious babe.

Lori touches her new haircut and squints at the mirror.

                    LORI
          Oh my God, I can't really see myself but
          I just feel better.

Lori puts on her coke bottle glasses and admires. Judy takes
them off.

The door opens. Scott's head pokes in.

                    SCOTT
          Hey Jude, wanna lose at..

Scott's eyes Lori. His mouth drops. He is speechless.

                    JUDY
          Knock, dude.

Judy pushes awestruck Scott out head first. Lori is ecstatic about his reaction.

                    JUDY (CONT'D)
          Your first victim.

                    LORI
          Thank you so much! I've got to go now.
          Dad will get worried.

                    JUDY
          Ok, see you tomorrow. Why don't you wear
          that?

                    LORI
          Can I!?

Lori gathers her things and exits. She bumps into the door.

                    LORI (CONT'D)
          Oops!

                    JUDY
          Contacts.

                    LORI
          Contacts.

Judy hands Lori her glasses.

INT. MARILYN'S HOUSE - EVENING

Tammy jumps up and down.

                    TAMMY
          Well what would you have done?

Marilyn calmly sprawls on the leather CHAISE LOUNGE of her garishly decorated home smoking thin cigarettes.

                    MARILYN
          You did the right thing by coming. Momma
          Marilyn will take care of it.

She exhales the smoke and puts out the cigarette.

INT. SWIMING POOL - EVENING

Marilyn talks with officer Skip over Jonas's body. She nervously smokes a cigarette nudging the corpse with her high heel.

                    SKIP
          Looks to me like ol' Jonas was working
          his sausage when the railing gave way.
          How does that sound for starters?

                    MARILYN
          He was always trying to dip his wick into
          my girls. But apparently what he lacked
          in brains, he made up for in other
          departments.

Marilyn floats her hankie over Jonas's Rigamortis penis.

                    SKIP
          I'll clean it up from here.

Marilyn stuffs a wad of bills in Skip's pocket and pats it.

                    MARILYN
          Good man.

INT. BIOLOGY CLASSROOM - MORNING

A student pats his shirt pocket and retrieves a CHEAT SHEET.

Students diligently take a multiple choice test, sitting two
to a table in the classical Biology classroom.

A school newspaper reads: BELOVED JANITOR DIES OF HEART
ATTACK. Tammy covers the headline with her book and looks
around the room.

Sean sits next to Judy and cheats off her paper. Mr. Sontag
paces the room. Ryan cheats off Lori's paper.
Unbespectacled Lori blinks conspicuously.

                    MR. SONTAG
          Ok, everybody, time's up.

Mr. Sontag walks around and picks up the student's tests. He
stops at Judy and Sean's table. He continues by Lori and is
baffled by her beauty. Ryan stares at Lori's breasts and
then at her new face.

                    MR. SONTAG (CONT'D)
          Just to keep everyone honest. I made
          sure each table had different tests.

Sean, Ryan and Trisha let out a MOAN. Mr. Sontag smiles
smugly at Sean.

                      MR. SONTAG (CONT'D)
And since we're studying other animal's
reproduction, I think it's a good time
for the sex education shoe box. Any
questions you are embarrassed about or
too afraid to ask your parents, just
write it here and don't sign your name.

The students giggle and qladly prepare their questions. Sean
and Ryan show each other theirs and slap a high five. The
shoe box is passed around as each deposits their questions.

Mr. Sontag picks up the box and prepares to read the first
scrap of paper.

                      MR. SONTAG (CONT'D)
Uh, Ok. Why does it burn when I pee?

The students ROAR in laughter.

                      MR. SONTAG (CONT'D)
Ok, class, quiet down.

Mr. Sontag lowers his raised hand.

                      MR. SONTAG (CONT'D)
It could be a simple urinary tract
infection, or the major symptom of a
sexually transmitted disease such as
gonorrhea or syphilis.

Mr. Sontag casually glances at Trisha who immediately looks
at her note book and starts scribbling. Ryan looks over to
Trisha and glares.

                      MR. SONTAG (CONT'D)
Regardless, you should get it checked out
by a doctor right away.

Mr. Sontag reaches back into the box and retrieves another
scrap.

                      MR. SONTAG (CONT'D)
O..k. Sorry you feel that way.

He scrunches the paper; looks at Ryan and reaches back into
the box. He becomes agitated as he reads it.

                      MR. SONTAG (CONT'D)
Hmmm. I don't know. Why don't you ask
your mother this one?

Mr. Sontag puts the unfolded note in front of Sean that
reads:

WHAT DOES IT FEEL LIKE TO GET FUCKED IN THE ASS

Judy glances over, reads the notes and covers her mouth to
stop from laughing out loud. She beams at Mr. Sontag for his
boldness. He proudly returns her smile.

Sean is angry and looks around at Ryan who snickers at Sean's
foiled question.

                    MR. SONTAG (CONT'D)
          Ok, next question.

Mr. Sontag unfolds the next scrap.

                    MR. SONTAG (CONT'D)
          How do you know when you're in love?

Mr. Sontag smiles at the new Lori who blushes red. The bell
RINGS.

                    MR. SONTAG (CONT'D)
          That's a tough one .

The class gets ready to disperse.

                    MR. SONTAG (CONT'D)
          Read chapter 12 and do the questions at
          the end of the chapter.

Students file out the door. Ryan punches angry Sean in the
arm who looks back annoyed. Lori gives a cute wave to Mr.
Sontag who admires back. Judy lingers.

                    JUDY
          Nice work Mr. Sontag.

                    MR. SONTAG
          You can call me Terry when no one is
          around.

                    JUDY
          You crack me up.

                    MR. SONTAG
          Say, I couldn't help noticing your RRR
          box.

Judy holds it up.

                    JUDY
          Want a piece of gum?

                    MR. SONTAG
          No,(nervous laugh) I didn't think you
          would be the kind to join.

                    JUDY
          Insecure, lame and mean?

Judy laughs. Mr. Sontag sadly smiles.

                    MR. SONTAG
          I had a girlfriend once in Triple R.

                    JUDY
          You did?

                    MR. SONTAG
          We were madly in love. We were going to
          get married after CMSU. She even got a
          scholarship.

                    JUDY
          Where is she now?

                    MR. SONTAG
          Dead.

                    JUDY
          Oh...I'm so sorry. What happened? If you
          don't mind me asking.

                    MR. SONTAG
          She killed herself.

Judy puts her hand over her mouth.

                    JUDY
          Oh my God, why?

                    MR. SONTAG
          I wish I knew. It was just after she
          became an "officer" and 3 weeks later she
          just changed.

Judy squeezes his hand.

                    MR. SONTAG (CONT'D)
          They found her too late. She took all
          her mother's sleeping pills. All she
          left was a note that said "forgive me".

Mr. Sontag eyes well with tears.

                    MR. SONTAG (CONT'D)
          I wish I knew what I was supposed to
          forgive. She was wonderful. She looks a
          bit like Lori does now, and sweet and
          caring. Did you do that?

                    JUDY
          Yup.

                    MR. SONTAG
          I thought so.

Trisha walks by the door and stares at the two. Mr. Sontag
notices Trisha, gets nervous and stands up straight.

                    MR. SONTAG (CONT'D)
          So there's the answer to your question.
          We'll see you tomorrow.

                    JUDY
          Ok, see you tomorrow...Mr. Sontag.

Judy walks out to Trisha.

                    TRISHA
          What did he want?

                    JUDY
          Oh, nothing.

INT. HIGH SCHOOL GYNASIUM - EVENING

Students mill around the cheaply decorated gymnasium. Judy
stands near the now beautiful Lori. People stop and stare.
Lori blinks conspicuously, shy of her new found celebrity.

                    JUDY
          Head up, shoulders straight and smile.

Lori complies.

                    JUDY (CONT'D)
          Try not to blink for 20 seconds.

Lori makes her eyes wide.

                    LORI
          I'll be right back.

Lori walks toward the punch bowl with her eyes still wide.
Judy sighs, trying to be patient. Mitch swoops out of
nowhere.

                    MITCH
          Missed you at the bonfire.

                    JUDY
          Yeah?

                    MITCH
          Sorry to hear about your little accident.

Mitch makes a fluttering motion with his fingers.

Judy nods.

                    MITCH (CONT'D)
          I was wondering if I, uh, well, if I
          could show you, I mean sometime, when
          you're not busy, some of the finer spots
          of Jeff City.

Judy cocks her head.

                    JUDY
          Sometime would be fine.

                    MITCH
          8 o'clock next Friday?

                    JUDY
          Eight's great.

Lori returns with punch and hands one to Judy.

                    MITCH
          Hi, uh..

                    LORI
          Lori.

                    MITCH
          See you girls later.

Lori squeezes Judy's arm hard.

                    LORI
          Mitch Northway was talking to you!

                    JUDY
          Owww.

Marilyn walks on stage, grabs the microphone and begins
talking over the loud crowd.

                    MARILYN
          Now, the moment you've all been waiting
          for.

No one responds or listens. She jerks the microphone and
forces it to purposely scream FEEDBACK. The students grab
for their ears. She feigns innocence.

                    MARILYN (CONT'D)
          Oh...pardon me.

She fumbles to open an envelope.

                    MARILYN (CONT'D)
          Your King and Queen of Jefferson City
          High School are....

Marilyn rips at the envelope.

Trisha springs away from Sean and Ryan smiling coquettishly
back at them, straightening her hair. Marilyn doesn't even
bother to look at the card.

                    MARILYN (CONT'D)
          Miss Tammy Gibson and Mitch Northway.

Trisha lunges forward and is hugged by Tammy and then pushed
away. Tammy bounds on stage. Trisha is in shock. Tammy
motions for Mitch to join her. He shrugs modestly and
complies.

Kay looks on from the side stage and wipes a tear. Marilyn
trots over to Kay.

                    KAY
          Thank you so much.

                    MARILYN
          It was the least I could do.

Kay embraces Marilyn.

                    MARILYN (CONT'D)
          Not in front of everyone.

They both clap toward the audience. A girl CROWNS Tammy.

Trisha crosses her arms and ignores the pleadings of Ryan and
Sean. Trisha storms away. Mitch stares in to the audience
at Judy. He smiles and shrugs. Judy covers her mouth to keep
from laughing at the odd scene.

INT. JUDY'S FAMILY ROOM - MORNING

Joan helps angry Judy fix a hankie on her hair as she puts the finishing touches on her baby wear. A pacifier hangs around her neck. Scott looks on with his arms folded, smirking.

                    JOAN
          Oh honey, I think you look adorable--

                    SCOTT
          --Hysterical.

A horn HONKS outside.

                    JOAN
          Wait, wait. Let me take a picture first.

Joan readies her camera as Judy stands annoyed. Scott laughs and makes a face. Judy coyly flips Scott the bird as the camera FLASHES.

                    JOAN (CONT'D)
          Great!

Judy and Scott chuckle and shake their heads. Joan looks out the window.

                    JOAN (CONT'D)
          You have a great time, honey.

                    SCOTT
          Don't forget this!

Scott hands Judy a baby bottle and falls on the couch laughing. Judy bites the tip of the bottle;spits it at Scott and heads out the door.

EXT. JUDY'S HOUSE- NOON

Judy gets in Trisha's purple Monza in front of the large Ranch style brick home. Scott looks out the window for one more yuck. Judy smooths her eyebrow with her "bird" finger at Scott. Trisha is in a foul mood.

INT. TRISHA'S BASEMENT - AFTERNOON

Judy and 10 other baby dressed hopefuls stand in a line in front of 20 members who sit sneering at the pledges. Lori stands next to Judy excitedly.

                              LORI
                         (to Judy)
                    I thought there was no way, and all of a
                    sudden, I got an invite. I know it's
                    because of you.

Judy takes a suck off her baby bottle like it's whiskey.

                              JUDY
                    This is un-fucking believable. Nobody
                    would believe me if I told them back
                    home.

                              LORI
                    Isn't it great!

Judy rolls her eyes.

                              TRISHA
                    Quiet! Ok, so, we have you dressed like
                    this because, just like a baby, you don't
                    know anything.

Trisha points to a girl dressed only in a baby bonnet
whispering.

                              TRISHA (CONT'D)
                    You...out! When I say to do something,
                    you do it!

The girl starts to cry.

                              TRISHA (CONT'D)
                    That's right, now you're acting like a
                    baby.

The devastated girl looks earnestly at Trisha believing she's
been forgiven.

                              TRISHA (CONT'D)
                    I said out!

Trisha points to the door.

The girl continues to bawl and heads out the door. Her life
is over.

                              TRISHA (CONT'D)
                    Here are your pledge books. Read them,
                    love them, live them.

Trisha smiles and pauses handing Judy her pledge book.
Trisha thrusts a book in disgust at Lori who excitedly opens
it and begins to read it.

>   TRISHA (CONT'D)
>   All interests of the club, must be kept
>   within the club. No exceptions!

Judy looks bored and unenthused.

>   TRISHA (CONT'D)
>   When you see a member, you must approach
>   her and call her Miss. If you don't, 50
>   cent fine. You must also offer her a
>   piece of gum and to carry her books. Too
>   many fines is cause for probation. Am I
>   clear?

>   GIRLS
>   Yes!

Judy stands insolently,arms crossed. Trisha looks at Judy's
blank face.

>   TRISHA
>   The rest of the rules of your pledgeship
>   are contained in your books. Any
>   questions?

The girls look intent.

>   TRISHA (CONT'D)
>   Good, and if anyone asks you the secret
>   meaning of Triple R, what do you say?

>   GIRLS
>   (in unison)
>   Really, rather, ristocratic.

Trisha revels in her power.

>   TRISHA
>   Excellent, until you know the real
>   meaning. If you make it that far.

Trisha glares at Judy.

>   TRISHA (CONT'D)
>   Lemonade and cookies are in the next
>   room.

>   JUDY
>   (to herself)
>   I need a beer.

>   LORI
>   Judy, it says right here, no drinking.

Judy takes Lori's finger out of her pledge book and closes it for her as they walk into the next room.

INT. KAY'S APARTMENT - AFTERNOON

Kay sits on a floral couch in her 80's to-the-max apartment, finishing off the end of a bottle of wine. A box of Bon-bons and a PERSONAL FACE MASSAGER, shaped suspiciously phallic, rest on the table.

Tammy enters and slams the door. She beelines for the telephone and dials.

                    KAY
          Baby, be a love and get momma fresh
          glass.

                    TAMMY
          Get it yourself.

Kay turns around.

                    KAY
          How's that new Dawson girl?

                    TAMMY
          Still perfect.

Kay gets up to fill her own glass.

                    KAY
          I brought her mother over some of that
          old frozen sausage from Gerbes to fatten
          her up to even out the squad.

Kay pinches and slaps Tammy's thigh making it jiggle.

                    TAMMY
          Momma!

Tammy bats her mom's hands away.

                    KAY
          Well, girls your age aren't supposed to
          have the cottage cheese yet.

                    TAMMY
          You're no skinny minny.

Tammy grabs one of Kay's gut rolls through her silk shirt and twists in anger.

                KAY
      Ow! You little bitch.

Kay jumps away. Tammy goes to the boxes on the table.

              TAMMY
      What is this shit?!

              KAY
      They are new Jenny Craig meals. These
      jelly rolls are gonna melt away.

Kay sucks in her gut.

              TAMMY
      If you got off your back once in a while,
      you wouldn't have that problem.

              KAY
      Well, looks whose talking. Listen little
      missy, don't you forget who puts a roof
      over your head and meals on those thighs.

Kay walks into the kitchen and feigns weeping. Tammy follows
behind her.

              TAMMY
      Momma, I'm sorry.

Tammy puts her head on her shoulder.

              KAY
      Ever since your father died.

              TAMMY
      I know. Momma, tell me about him again.

Kay grabs a 60's style picture of a very handsome man in a
frame and dusts it off.

              KAY
      He loved you so much baby. Then, the
      hurricane and his private yacht. I don't
      want to talk about it.

              TAMMY
      It's OK momma.

Tammy exits, grabbing a seam ripper and needle off the
counter, kissing Kay on the cheek.

Kay looks over her shoulder, her face turns blank. She
carelessly tosses the picture on the counter and begins to
put away the groceries.

> KAY
> (singing a la Janis Joplin)
> Oh Lord, won't you buy me a Mercedes
> Benz...

INT. JUDY'S FAMILY ROOM

Judy, still wearing some remnants of her baby costume, talks
on the phone with Scott in the background.

> JUDY
> Me too Mitch. Just honk.

Judy swaggers side to side and smiles.

> JUDY (CONT'D)
> Bye.

She hangs up.

> SCOTT
> So you landed a date with Mitch Northway!
> I can't believe it. My days of towel
> whippings in gym class are over!

> JUDY
> It's just a date.

Judy toys with the phone.

> SCOTT
> With the emperor. You like him?

> JUDY
> What's wrong with that?

Scott lays back on the couch.

> SCOTT
> Nothing. Does he have a sister?

> JUDY
> I think they're older, but I'm sure we
> can line something up for you. What
> about Lori?

> SCOTT
> Before or after your Teen magazine
> makeover?

> JUDY
> And you are *so* hot. Beggars can't be
> choosers. Out! I've got Bio to do.

                    SCOTT
          For Son-fag.

                    JUDY
          It's Sontag, and I wouldn't listen to
          what people say.

Judy walks by and flicks him in the ear. She turns off the
TV and leaves.

                    SCOTT
          Hey!

INT. MARILYN'S OFFICE - AFTERNOON

                    MARILYN
          Hi Chet.

INT. CAPITOL BUILDING OFFICE

                    CHET
          Well hello my dear.

INTERCUT AS NEEDED

                    MARILYN
          Good news! She's rushing!

                    CHET
          Already heard. How'd you do it?

                    MARILYN
          Never you mind, and it's not all done
          yet.

                    CHET
          Ol' Santa gonna be coming down a few
          virgin chimneys--

                    MARILYN
          --It's a wonder you all keep getting
          elected.

Chet walks into the bathroom holding his cordless phone. He
flips up the toilet seat and arrogantly unzips his pants.

                    CHET
          You give the people what they want, they
          keep coming back--

                    MARILYN
          --or those ballot boxes keep getting
          stuffed.
                         (MORE)

Using state money to keep your sex life
afire ain't exactly helping the folks in
your district.

                    CHET
The state charitable distribution fund
has a broad definition.

                    CHET (CONT'D)
Aiyeeeearggghh!

                    MARILYN
Relax.

                    CHET
Goddammit Marilyn, I think that little
bitch Trisha gave me the clap. I knew
it!

                    MARILYN
Now calm down. She has an appointment
with the good doctor tomorrow.

                    CHET
A lot of good that does me now. Damnit.

Chet zips up his pants.

                    CHET (CONT'D)
Tammy was my first choice anyway. She
hasn't been slutting around too, has she?

                    MARILYN
I thought she was with your buddy from
district 4.

                    CHET
Fuck him. I'm the one who puts my ass on
the line for this.

                    MARILYN
Now Chet, you better just take a week
off. You remember what happened during
the last outbreak.

Chet looks at his crotch.

                    CHET
If you'd a kept a closer watch on your
girls.

                    MARILYN
Now Chet.

CLICK, Marilyn stares at the phone.

                    MARILYN (CONT'D)
          My, my, my the manners on that boy.

Marilyn dials the phone again.

                    MARILYN (CONT'D)
          Kay, girl how you been?

INT. KAY'S LIVING ROOM - AFTERNOON

Kay lays drunken on her flowered couch watching "All My
Children" slowly dissecting Bonbons with her teeth.

                    KAY
          I was meaning to call and thank you for
          the latest installment.

INTERCUT AS NEEDED

                    MARILYN
          No problem honey, you earned it. It seems
          Miss Trisha's been playing hokey pokey
          with a rotten dokey and gave ol' Chet the
          screaming pee pees.

                    KAY
          Woo! Uh huh. Well it serves that selfish
          bastard right.

                    MARILYN
          The reason I'm calling is, err, I know
          you asked me not to.

                    KAY
          You keep that bastard away from my baby!

                    MARILYN
          He's asked for her.

Kay jerks up alarmed and sober and looks to the bedroom.

                    KAY
          Well get him the next girl. I don't need
          her leaving an infected snail trail on my
          toilet seat.

                    MARILYN
          I'll see what I can do.

                    KAY
          Thank you girl. I don't ask for much.
          Speak of the devil woman.

Tammy, dressed in her cheerleading uniform, slams the door
and leaves. Kay lays back down.

                    MARILYN
          Ok baby, put me down for another box of
          detergent and some of that face cream.

Kay hangs up and grabs the wine bottle brushing by her
personal massager. It accidentally turns on and VIBRATES.

EXT. HIGH SCHOOL TRACK INFIELD - AFTERNOON

Judy, Tammy, Trisha and Becky practice their cheers while the
football team scrimmages. Tammy, wearing the homecoming
CROWN, is completely consumed in her form feeling very
important. The girls high kick.

Judy wears shorts underneath her skirt. Mitch tosses the
football back and forth and looks at Judy after each throw.

Much younger girls practice their cheers nearby in awe of the
older girls.

Mitch keeps Judy's gaze and throws the football horribly off
course hitting the COACH (50) in the butt. He reels around.
Judy laughs.

                    COACH
          Northway! Damn you boy, get over here!

 Mitch heads towards the coach.

                    BECKY
               (to Trisha)
          That girl better watch it.

                    TRISHA
          What's it gonna take for her to learn her
          lesson.

Trisha looks at Judy in anger, and gets even more enraged
when she sees Tammy reveling in her crown.

                    TAMMY
          Come on you guys, this is important!
          Watch how good I am at this. You've
          really got to get your legs (pant) high
          (pant) and point your toes.

Tammy kicks and points with one leg, alternating to the
other.

                    TAMMY (CONT'D)
          Really high!

Tammy kicks her leg so vigorously, she pulls her other leg
out from underneath her and falls. Judy laughs. Becky and
Trisha start to laugh but stop when they catch Tammy's death
glare. Mrs. Weir approaches.

                    MARILYN
          You're not setting a very good example
          for our future cheerleaders.

Marilyn fondles the hair of a 8-year-old girl at her side.

EXT. HIGH SCHOOL PARKING LOT - AFTERNOON

The girls walk to their cars carrying their gear.

Lori Brown hurries up to Tammy and Trisha.

                    LORI
          Hello, Miss Tammy, Miss Trisha. Would
          you like a piece of gum?

Lori opens her decorated cigar BOX full of gum.

                    TRISHA
          Sure.

Trisha takes a piece and throws the wrapper back in. Lori
presents it to Tammy who clears out her box with a huge
handful and throws the gum in her purse.

                    LORI
          Oh, ok. Is there anything else I can do
          for you?

                    TAMMY
          Yeah, lay down on the ground and fry like
          a piece of bacon.

Trisha sneers.

                    LORI
          Oh, you guys are so funny.

Lori SNORTS.

                    TAMMY
          I mean it. Drop those books and get on
          the ground or you're history!

Lori quickly puts her books down and gets on her knees.

                    LORI
          Like this?

                    TAMMY
          You ever seen a piece of bacon with
          knees? All the way!

Lori lies down, face first on the asphalt.

                    TAMMY (CONT'D)
          Start sizzlin!

Lori starts to slowly convulse and makes HISSING noises as
Trisha and Tammy laugh and get in Trisha's Monza. They
drive off as Lori continues to sizzle.

Judy crouches to Lori.

                    JUDY
          You still want to be in this?

Lori continues to sizzle.

                    LORI
          Oh yes, sizzle,sizzle.

                    JUDY
          You can get up now, they're gone.

Judy dusts off Lori.

                    JUDY (CONT'D)
          Need a ride?

                    LORI
          That would be great.

                    JUDY
          You just can't let people treat you like
          that.

                    LORI
          But I'm a pledge.

                    JUDY
          This is going to change.

INT. JUDY'S BEDROOM

Judy talks on the phone.

                    JUDY
          It's like people are nice to them because
          they're afraid of them.

EXT. BARB'S BACKYARD

Barb paints her toenails.

> BARB
> Well, see you can't quit. These other
> girls need you. You love projects! And
> we get to Part-ee! Everybody wins.

> JUDY
> I guess so.

> BARB
> And you are going to be the cutest
> cowgirl ever!

INT. LIVING ROOM - DAY

Judy, Scott, Joan and Kirk stand in the living room putting
the finishing touches on Judy's tight blue-jeaned western
wear.

> KIRK
> Don't forget this.

Kirk crowns Judy's head with a cowboy hat as Joan ties a
bandana around her neck. A HONK sounds.

> JOAN
> Don't be too late honey.

> JUDY
> I'll try not to.

EXT. BRICK HOUSE

Judy gets in Trisha's Monza. Kirk stands at the door with
Joan and Scott. Judy wants to crawl in a hole.

> KIRK
> Ya'all come back now ya hear?

> JUDY
> Dad.

Kirk, Joan and Scott wave at Judy as she drives away
embarrassed.

EXT. PARKING LOT

The Triple R girls wash several cars, playing around,
throwing sponges at each other. Nearly all are dressed in
white t-shirts, many in daisy-duke cutoffs.

Judy and Lori towel dry a Toyota Corolla.

Chet drives up in his CADILLAC ELDORADO. Tammy and Becky race up to him. Trisha shyly stays back. Chet takes the hose from Tammy and sprays down several girls as they squeal, apparently too dumb to run away. This of course reveals their young and supple breasts.

>   CHET
>   You like that, huh.

Judy creeps out while observing the scene and puts her Western shirt back on.

INT. TRISHA'S BASEMENT - EVENING

Girls mill around in cow skirts, blue jean shirts and hats. Tammy is now drunk, swinging a lasso over her head. She snags a petite girl.

>   TAMMY
>   WOO! Got one.

Tammy jerks the lasso tight jerking the pledge toward her, sending the pledge to the ground.

>   TRISHA
>   Ok girls, we have an announcement.

Trisha unlassoes the pledge and abruptly motions Tammy to the corner.

>   TRISHA (CONT'D)
>   I'd like to declare our newest officer,
>   Sherry Watson.

SHERRY gleams with pride bouncing her short feathered hair. The other girls pat her on the back. Tammy staggers up and puts the lasso over Sherry's body and tightens it.

>   TAMMY
>   You're going to love being an officer.
>   You get to do a lot of them.

Trisha pulls Tammy away.

>   TRISHA
>   You better watch it sister.

>   TAMMY
>   Oh, relax.

>   TRISHA
>   Pull your shit together.

Tammy stands erect like a soldier and then relaxes into laughing. Trisha bristles towards Sherry to remove the lasso.

                    TRISHA (CONT'D)
          Congratulations sister.

Trisha pins a special yellow officer RIBBON on Sherry's blouse.

                    TRISHA (CONT'D)
          Tonight, we celebrate and teach you the
          ropes.

A car HONKS.

                    JUDY
          That's my ride. Gotta go. See you girls
          later.

Judy zips out the door.

                    TRISHA
          Where does she think she's going? We
          decide when the meeting is over.

                    TAMMY
          Looks like your losing your grip.

Tammy plays with the lasso.

Trisha opens the curtains to see Mitch's black redone '57 Chevy truck and Judy climbing into it. Trisha whips the curtains closed.

                    TAMMY (CONT'D)
          What is it?

                    TRISHA
          Nothing.

Tammy opens the curtains. Tammy falls to the floor in a SHRIEK.

                    TAMMY
               (bawling)
          My Mitch!

Trisha comforts Tammy.

                    TRISHA
          Baby, you know you're better than her.
          He'll tire of her and be back for you in
          no time.

                         TAMMY
              No he won't.

Tammy gets up to run out the door. Trisha stands in front of
the door.

                         TRISHA
              He's not worth it.

                         TAMMY
              He is too.

Tammy forcefully pushes Trisha to the ground and starts out
the door.

                         TAMMY (CONT'D)
              MITCH! MITCH!

Mitch's truck is 100 feet away.

INT. BLACK CHEVY TRUCK - EVENING

Mitch and Judy smile and giggle. Mitch notices Tammy
flailing after him in his rear view and loses his smile.
Trisha comes outside with the lasso and expertly rings Tammy
jerking her to the ground. Mitch starts laughing.

                         JUDY
              What's so funny?

                         MITCH
              Nothing.

EXT. FRONT LAWN - EVENING

Tammy wrestles to get back up.

                         TAMMY
              Let me go, you bitch. He needs me.

                         TRISHA
              You're not going anywhere little piggy.

Trisha finishes hog tieing Tammy.

INT. BLACK CHEVY TRUCK - DAY

                         MITCH
              You look great!

                         JUDY
              Thanks.

Judy takes off her cowboy hat and flannel shirt to reveal a soft white T-shirt.

The majestic state capitol BUILDING looms in the foreground.

                    MITCH
          So the capitol building was modeled after
          the one in Washington D.C..

                    JUDY
          Cool.

Judy just stares and smiles at Mitch.

                    MITCH
          Yeah, cool.

Mitch nods at Judy and pulls to a GRAVEL PAD over looking the river.

                    MITCH (CONT'D)
          So you see that bluff way over there, and
          this one we're on?

                    JUDY
          Yeah.

                    MITCH
          The river used to be that wide.

Mitch spreads his arms and coyly puts his arm around Judy and snuggles closer.

                    MITCH (CONT'D)
          Until they channelled it for the river
          boats so they wouldn't hit ground.

Mitch pulls her closer as part of his explanation.

                    JUDY
          Neat.

                    MITCH
          Yeah, neat.

Mitch plants a sensual kiss on Judy.

                    MITCH (CONT'D)
          So are you starting to like it here a
          little more?

                    JUDY
          Yeah, I guess so.

Mitch kisses Judy again.

>   JUDY (CONT'D)
>   A lot more.

Mitch gently rubs her breast. He lowers his hand to her
zipper.

>   JUDY (CONT'D)
>   Not so fast buster.

>   MITCH
>   Ok.

>   JUDY
>   The girls here might be that easy but I'm
>   not.

>   MITCH
>   The girls here.

Mitch pulls back.

>   MITCH (CONT'D)
>   If you wouldn't walk around talking about
>   how great California is all the time,
>   maybe you'd get to know a few of them.

Judy is alarmed that he is so annoyed.

>   MITCH (CONT'D)
>   And I'm not talking about Tammy and
>   Trisha. Shit, they're probably just
>   using you to make themselves look better.
>   Why are you in that group anyway?

>   JUDY
>   So everyone will like me, isn't it
>   working?

Judy smiles.

>   MITCH
>   No, for real.

>   JUDY
>   For one, my parents made me.

>   MITCH
>   How'd they "make" you.

>   JUDY
>   Plane ticket.

>   MITCH
>   Dont tell me. Back to California.

Mitch hits the steering wheel.

>   JUDY
>   Well have you ever been?

>   MITCH
>   No. But what I do know is that wherever
>   you're from, people are the same deep
>   down.

>   JUDY
>   I agree.

>   MITCH
>   Even Tammy and Trisha.

Judy raises her eyebrow.

>   MITCH (CONT'D)
>   Ok, really deep down sometimes.

They both laugh. Mitch's anger is gone.

>   MITCH (CONT'D)
>   Is my princess ready to cruise the
>   boulevard?

>   JUDY
>   Yes ma lord.

>   MITCH
>   Well come with me my lady. California's
>   got nothing on us.

Mitch starts up his truck.

EXT. MISSOURI BOULEVARD - LATE EVENING

Throngs of cars ooze down the four lane road speckled with
monster lighted signs like McDonalds, Hardees and Mid-
Missouri Lanes.

INT. BLACK CHEVY TRUCK

Mitch waves at several people in the opposing lanes who honk
and catch his attention. Judy waves back to a few familiar
faces.

>   MITCH
>   See, it's not so bad.

Judy sips her McDonalds soda admiring Mitch.

                    JUDY
          No, it's not.

She smiles out the window as they gently rock to the radio.
(suggest Reo Speedwagon)

Mitch suddenly attempts to change lanes and looks annoyed.
He can't move from the center lane.

                    JUDY (CONT'D)
          What's the matter?

                    MITCH
          Just a little road hazard.

Judy notices Trisha's Monza slowly approaching packed with
Becky in front. Sherry and Tammy are stuffed in the back.
Judy sits up high and waves at Trisha and Becky who wave
back. Tammy tries to climb to the front seat.

INT. PURPLE MONZA

                    TAMMY
          Mitch! Mitch!

Trisha face claws Tammy and stuffs her back in the seat.

INT. BLACK CHEVY TRUCK

                    MITCH
          Oh God.

                    JUDY
          How long did you and Tammy date?

                    MITCH
          I wouldn't call it dating.

Judy shakes her head.

                    MITCH (CONT'D)
          I mean, I may have gotten a...you know...

Mitch bucks his hips and pushes an imaginary head to his
crotch continuing to drive.

                    MITCH (CONT'D)
          But I would only make love with someone
          that I loved.

                    JUDY
          So am I one of these?

Judy mimics Mitch's action.

                    MITCH
          Guess that was kind of rude wasn't it?

                    JUDY
          Yeah.

                    MITCH
          No, I think you are the real thing.

                    JUDY
          So you've never even practiced?

                    MITCH
          Not yet. I've got a reputation to
          uphold.

Mitch smiles and pulls over to the bluff. Judy realizes he's
serious.

                    MITCH (CONT'D)
          Tammy thinks because I'm the Quarterback
          and she's the head cheerleader that--

                    JUDY
          --she's supposed to give you head.

Mitch tries not to laugh.

                    MITCH
          I've known her since grade school. She's
          like my--

                    JUDY
          --Oooh, don't even say it.

Judy and Mitch laugh.

                    MITCH
          You got me...and I know you don't believe
          me. But I've never been in love. But I
          think that it might be just around the
          corner.

Mitch earnestly scoots towards Judy, gently kissing her,
letting her believe she's in charge.

INT. PURPLE MONZA

The girls sit smashed in their car passing around "Tickle
Pink" wine. Suggest AC/DC "Highway to Hell". Tammy tokes on
a joint.

                         TAMMY
                    (inhaled)
               If that bitch hadn't moved to town, he'd
               be all mine.

She exhales and passes it.

                         TAMMY (CONT'D)
               And after all we've done for her.

                         TRISHA
               Yeah, we've been the real fucking welcome
               wagon.

Becky giggles.

                         TAMMY
               So Sherry, next week at that big
               Christmas party, if one of the old
               codgers wants a little something extra.
               Think about it.

                         SHERRY
               Ewww!

Trisha cups her earlobe to show her earring.

                         SHERRY (CONT'D)
               Those are beautiful! Did you?.. Oh.

                         TRISHA
               And whatever you do, you can tell no one,
               and I mean no one. Is that clear?

                         SHERRY
               Clear.

                         TRISHA
               Only at officer meetings.

Sherry struggles to justify it in her mind.

                         SHERRY
               I knew Sally Ann Craze was too dumb to
               get that scholarship to Mizzou.

Tammy rocks out in the back seat pulling her hair over her
face. Trisha reaches into her purse and uncaps a
PRESCRIPTION BOTTLE and takes a pill. Becky tries to read the
bottle but Trisha buries it deep in her purse.

INT. BLACK CHEVY TRUCK

Judy and Mitch sit parked in front of Judy's house.

                    MITCH
          So it's just you two, huh? I'll have to
          look out for him.

                    JUDY
          Yeah, he's a piece of work. He thinks
          you're a god.

                    MITCH
          He does?

Mitch smiles at the house.

                    MITCH (CONT'D)
          Do you?

                    JUDY
          I don't think I'm up to God yet, but..

Mitch pulls Judy closer and kisses her. The porch light
flicks ON and off and ON again.

                    MITCH
          I'll call you tomorrow.

                    JUDY
          Deal.

Judy kisses him one more time and hops out of the truck.

INT. FOYER - LATE EVENING

Judy enters and closes the door.

                    SCOTT
               (singing)
          K-I-S-S-I-N-G. First comes love...

                    JUDY
          Then comes Judy kicking Scott's ass.
          That was you turning on the porch light.

Judy karate flips laughing Scott flat-backed to the floor and
stands on his chest.

                    SCOTT
          I give. How'd it go?

                    JUDY
          Good, but would you shut up you're gonna
          wake up Mom and Dad.

                    SCOTT
          Impossible.

Scott pistons one finger inside the cylindricated other palm.

                    SCOTT (CONT'D)
          They were eeee..uh..eee..uh for like 2
          hours. They're sleeping like babies.

                    JUDY
          Oh my god, they are so old. I don't want
          to hear about that.

A KNOCK on the door. Judy leaves Scott on the floor and
opens the door to find Mitch holding a FOOTBALL.

Mitch looks over to Scott on the floor and tosses him the
football.

                    MITCH
          Hey bud, stop by before the game and
          we'll throw it around.

Mitch kisses thankful Judy one more time and waves goodbye to
awestruck smiling Scott on the ground.

                    SCOTT
          By far the coolest guy you've ever boned.

Judy quickly walks over Scott's chest and continues away.

EXT. FOOTBALL STADIUM -FRIDAY EVENING

The football game is in full-swing.

Score board reads Jeff City 21, Joplin 14. Judy, Tammy,
Trisha and Becky have just finished their cheer and are
kicking high waving their pom-poms. Scott, Kirk and Joan
wave at Judy. Judy smiles back at them.

The center hikes the ball to Mitch. No one is open and Mitch
decides to run it himself. A behemoth PLAYER tackles Mitch
low and stays on top of him. The fans let out an OOOH.

EXT. FOOTBALL FIELD -EVENING

Mitch lays under the giant.

                    MITCH
          My leg! My leg! Get off me...shit.

The player leans on Mitch to get up. Mitch winces in pain
grabbing his leg even more. Coaches run on the field.

                    MITCH (CONT'D)
          My leg.

                    COACH
          What in thee H-E double hockey sticks do
          you think you're doing running the ball
          boy. You're too valuable.

                    MITCH
          No one was open.

Mitch GASPS.

                    COACH
          And now look at you.

                    SEAN
          I can do it coach.

                    COACH
          Only thing you can do is run that mouth
          of yours, boy.

Judy runs up to Mitch who has a big smile for Judy through
his pain.

                    JUDY
          You OK?

                    MITCH
          Yeah, I'll be all right.

Mitch gasps.

                    COACH
          Get this dead meat off the field!

Coach looks around in disgust at his players.

                    COACH (CONT'D)
          Goddamnit! Sean you're it.

Tammy comes running up to Mitch still laying on the ground
and pushes Judy away. She smooths her hair behind her ear.

                    TAMMY
          Oh my God baby.

Mitch winces at the sight of her.

                    TAMMY (CONT'D)
          Does it hurt?

Tammy touches and squeezes the sweet spot.

                        MITCH
              YIKES! Shit! Somebody get her out of
              here!

Coach's assistants arrive with a gurney and push everyone out
of the way and load Mitch.

Judy covers her mouth.

                        TAMMY
              Baby, I'll come visit. I'll take care of
              you.

Mitch moans.

Tammy approaches Judy.

                        TAMMY (CONT'D)
              You know he's just using you.

Tammy huffs away back to the line up. Judy sighs at Tammy.

                        COACH
              Play ball!

Time passes. The game clock reads 2:30. Score Jeff City 21,
Joplin 41.

                        COACH (CONT'D)
              Damn that Northway boy.

Sean throws the ball. It is immediately intercepted and run
50 yards for another touchdown.

The cheerleaders are tired. Tammy ignores Judy. Judy rolls
her eyes and smiles to the neutral Trisha and Becky, who are
beginning to warm to her. Judy's eye is caught by Chet
giving a playful wave towards her as he hits his buddies and
laughs.

                        JUDY
                   (to Trisha)
              There's that letch again.

                        TRISHA
              That's Chet Carlson, only the biggest
              most powerful Representative in the
              state.

Trisha waves to Chet who doesn't reciprocate.

                        TRISHA (CONT'D)
              He can change your life.

Judy is creeped out.

Trisha adjusts her diamond earring.

>   TAMMY
>   (screaming)
>   We've got the power...to win--

>   TRISHA
>   --Give it up Tammy, we suck.

Judy and Becky giggle.

>   JUDY
>   What are you guys doing afterwards?

>   TRISHA
>   Well, uhm. We've got to go to this
>   thingie.

>   JUDY
>   Oh.

>   TRISHA
>   I'd invite you. I swear I would
>   but...it's only for officers. You
>   wouldn't want to do it anyway.

>   JUDY
>   No problem.

The game is over. The team trudges off the field, heads hanging low.

Chet comes down with his band of cronies and approaches the girls.

>   CHET
>   (to Team)
>   You'll get 'em next year boys.

Chet thrusts his hand to Judy and shakes.

>   CHET (CONT'D)
>   Chet Carlson, State of Missouri.
>   You're looking mighty fine out there.

>   JUDY
>   Uhm...thanks?

Tammy, Trisha and Becky are now talking with the other representatives. Judy observes.

                    JUDY (CONT'D)
          You guys sure are a friendly bunch.

                    CHET
          Just a little show-me state hospitality.

Chet opens his sport coat. Judy gives a pained smile.

                    JUDY
          We'll see you guys later, Ok?

                    CHET
          You coming tonight?

Judy is confused. Chet looks at Tammy and stops himself.

                    JUDY
          You girls have fun.

Trisha looks sad. Becky waves. Tammy flirts with a
legislator.

INT. GREEN STATION WAGON - EVENING

Kirk lets out Scott and Joan in front of their home. Judy
transfers to the front seat.

                    JOAN
          You give Mitch our best, sweetie.

                    SCOTT
          Yeah, our best.

Scott stands behind Joan and makes a BLOW JOB MOTION,
thrusting his tongue in his cheek, only for Judy to see.

                    JUDY
          I'll tell him it's from you Scott.

Scott stops. Big sister gets the last laugh again.

                    SCOTT
          Get Pepperoni!

                    KIRK
          OK.

Kirk drives away.

                    JUDY
          Thanks for taking me to see Mitch dad.

He pats her leg.

                    KIRK
          No problem sweetie.

Time passes.

Kirk pulls up to the small hospital, Judy exits.

                    JUDY
          Take your time.

Kirk smiles and drives away.

INT. HOSPITAL ROOM - EVENING

Mitch lies in bed surrounded by team members, his left leg
elevated.

Judy enters. Mitch's eyes light up.

                    MITCH
          Visiting time is over for you boys.
          Thanks for coming.

The players look at Judy and begin to SLAP high fives
goodbye.

                    SEAN
          See ya bud.

Judy smiles and nods at the exiting players.

                    JUDY
          So what did the doc say?

                    MITCH
          Torn ligaments, cartilage. I really
          screwed up.

                    JUDY
          I'm sorry.

Judy sits on the bed and combs his hair with her fingers.

                    JUDY (CONT'D)
          Does it hurt?

Judy plants a sensuous kiss on Mitch who excitedly
reciprocates.

                    MITCH
          Just right here.

Mitch touches his heart. Judy goes in to give him a kiss.

EXT. PIZZA PARLOR -EVENING

Kirk carries a pizza box and opens the door with one hand.
Kirk notices loud voices and turns around to see Tammy,
Trisha, Becky, Chet and other 40's-50's men in suits going in
to the log cabin style Moose Lodge.

                    KIRK
          I should be taking Judy to that.

Kirk notices Becky squeal with delight being goosed under her
skirt by a man.

                    KIRK (CONT'D)
          Oooh. Yikes.

Kirk raises his eyebrows, gets in his car and drives away.

INT. HOSPITAL ROOM - EVENING

Judy and Mitch continue to kiss. Judy recognizes her dad's
WHISTLING "Mack the Knife" and gets off the bed. Kirk
enters.

                    KIRK
          Hello Mitch.

                    MITCH
          Hello Mr. Dawson.

                    KIRK
          Fine game, until this.

                    MITCH
          Thank you, sir.

                    KIRK
          You ready to go pumpkin?

Judy squeezes Mitch's hand.

                    MITCH
          I'll talk to you tomorrow.

                    JUDY
          Definitely.

Judy and Kirk exit down the hallway.

INT. HALLWAY -EVENING

                    KIRK
          I saw Tammy and Trisha with their fathers
          going into the moose lodge to celebrate.

                    JUDY
          Tammy's dad is dead and Trisha's lives in
          Texas.

                    KIRK
          Hmmph.

INT. MOOSE LODGE -EVENING

Tammy, Trisha, Carolyn, Becky and Sherry are dressed in
bathing suits, drunk dancing on the small stage playing to
the raucous jeers of the legislators. Tammy bends over and
shakes her rump to a tan leisure suited man who playfully
spanks it. (Suggest "Flashlight" Parliament)

A man sprays Sherry with champagne. She loves it.

Chet jumps on stage. Tammy grabs his cocktail and downs it
with a laugh.

                    CHET
          Let's hear it for our "slap and
          ticklettes".

The crowd cheers. Officer Skip stands watch at the door.

Chet looks for a girl to put his arm around. Trisha smiles
but he chooses Tammy. Tammy waves at her regular man in the
crowd who waves back. Chet holds tighter.

                    CHET (CONT'D)
          And to our newest member, Sherry Watson.

The crowd cheers. Sherry gives a drunken wave.

                    SHERRY
          Hi Ya'all

Carolyn is roughly scooped off stage by her regular. She
strains a smile, but she is scared. Chet prowls Tammy but she
is swooped by her leisure suited regular.

                    TAMMY
           Hi big boy! Did you miss me?

Tammy gives him a drunken hug as he nods and feels her up.

Chet is pissed. He looks around to see Trisha meekly
smiling. Chet slams down his empty drink and storms off
stage. Trisha is approached by a new suited man. She folds
her arms and faintly smiles.

TIME PASSES

INT. PURPLE MONZA - NIGHT

Carolyn sobs rocking back and forth. Trisha comforts her.
Trisha smokes a cigarette with the door half-cocked.

                    CAROLYN
          I fucking quit!

Carolyn lights a cigarette showing her bruised face. Trisha
brushes the hair from her face.

                    CAROLYN (CONT'D)
          I said no Sedalia man, and who do I get,
          Sedalia man.

Carolyn looks in the vanity mirror.

                    CAROLYN (CONT'D)
          He doesn't want a girl, he wants a
          punching bag.

                    TRISHA
          I know hon. I'm not liking it either.

                    CAROLYN
          Then why do we do it?

                    TRISHA
          How else are you ever gonna be somebody?

The girls begrudgingly nod.

                    TRISHA (CONT'D)
          My "gina" is so sore.

Tammy stumbles out of a hotel room in front of their car.

                    TAMMY
          Hey girls!

Tammy pushes her way in the back seat behind Trisha getting a
glimpse of Carolyn.

                    TAMMY (CONT'D)
          I thought Sherry was getting Sedalia man.

Sherry looks stunned.

                    CAROLYN
          So did I. I quit.

                    TAMMY
          Now, now, now. Just stick it out a
          little while longer.
                    (MORE)

>   We're seniors and then we are set! I
>   think that one very handsome elected
>   official just might want to have babies
>   with me.

Tammy cocks her legs in the air, lying on her back.

>   TAMMY (CONT'D)
>   I told him I was on the pill

>   TRISHA
>   Liar.

Tammy smiles and lights a cigarette.

>   CAROLYN
>   You want your kids to do this?

>   TAMMY
>   Now Carolyn, you just got a bad one.
>   Trisha is pretty happy with her set up.

Tammy reaches up to fondle Trisha's ear. Trisha bats her
hand away which causes the earring to bounce off Carolyn's
lap and into the door jamb. Carolyn closes the door unaware
of the earring.

CRUNCH!

>   CAROLYN
>   Oh no.

Carolyn opens the door to discover her shattered earring.
She picks it up and observes it in her palm passing it to
Trisha.

>   CAROLYN (CONT'D)
>   I'm so sorry. They can fix it.

>   TRISHA
>   No they can't. I don't know much, but
>   this ain't no diamond, that sonuvabitch!

Trisha throws the remains out the door, removes the other one
and slams the door. Tammy cackles in the back seat.

>   TAMMY
>   It's the thought that counts.

Tammy roars with laughter. Trisha throws the other earring
at her.

>   TRISHA
>   Fuck you Tammy.

Trisha starts up the car and squeals away.

INT. MARILYN'S OFFICE - DAY

Marilyn and Tammy sit across from each other.

                    MARILYN
Tammy, I told you girl, show Chet special
attention and what do you do-go off with
that Rep. from Cape Giradeau.

                    TAMMY
He is que-oot. Chet...doesn't do it for
me.

                    MARILYN
And you went and told your momma all
about it.

                    TAMMY
Well.

                    MARILYN
She gave me an earful.

                    TAMMY
She ain't in charge of me and neither are
you.

                    MARILYN
You don't want me telling the truth about
ol' Jonas do you?

                    TAMMY
Oh all right.

Tammy spies Judy holding Mitch's books as he walks with
crutches, engrossed in playful conversation.

                    TAMMY (CONT'D)
And if this damn Triple R stuff wasn't
taking me away from my real man.

Tammy jumps up and runs out to Mitch and Judy.

INT. HALLWAY JEFFERSON CITY HIGH SCHOOL

                    TAMMY
I'll take those.

Tammy grabs the books out of Judy's hands. The books fly to
the floor.

Judy crouches down to help. Mitch stands annoyed.

                         JUDY
          Ok, can I just have my book back?

                         MITCH
          No. Tammy what the hell are you doing?

                         TAMMY
          I can do that for you sweetie.

                         MITCH
          No you can't.

Mitch bows down and winces in pain.

                         MITCH (CONT'D)
          Get the hell out of here.

Tammy throws the books back at Judy.

                         JUDY
          I'll see you at practice, ok?

                         TAMMY
          Not if I have anything to do with it.

Tammy storms off.

                         MITCH
          What was that supposed to mean?

                         JUDY
          Who knows.

Tammy grumbles down the hall. Trisha stands in front of her
holding an old magazine near the Library entrance.

                         TRISHA
          Oh my God. Check it out!

Trisha shows the same PICTURE of Tammy's dad we remember from
her kitchen. This time the MAGAZINE PHOTO shows him in a
SHAVING CREME AD.

                         TAMMY
          Let me see that!

                         TRISHA
          He was a model too!? You never told me
          that.

                         TAMMY
          Momma!

Tammy grabs the magazine and storms out the door.

                    TRISHA
          You better not mess that up. That's
          under my card.

INT. KAY'S LIVING ROOM - DAY

Kay still lays on the couch, tapping her personal massager on
her cheek. Tammy barges in holding the magazine and storms
to the kitchen.

                    KAY
          Well, hey baby. What you doing home from
          school so soon? Wanna join me for a
          taste?

Tammy re-enters with her Dad's picture FRAME in hand. She
throws the magazine down and takes off the back of the frame
and removes the flimsy picture.

                    TAMMY
          I knew it. You liar!

                    KAY
          Now Tammy, honey. I can explain.

                    TAMMY
          How daddy was a shaving cream model first
          before he got lost at sea.

                    KAY
          How'd you know?

Tammy hurls the frame at Kay.

                    TAMMY
          I'm through listening to you.

Tammy storms to her room and returns with a pile of clothes
on hangers.

                    KAY
          Where do you think you're going?

                    TAMMY
          Away from you!

Kay glares at her with disgust.

                    KAY
          You ain't got nowhere to go.

Kay lies back down.

                    TAMMY
          I know people who will take care of me.

Tammy pulls off Kay's blond bouffant wig to reveal Kay's
bobby-pinned matted brown hair. Tammy taunts Kay bouncing
the wig by her personal MASSAGER, like a head on a stick.

                    KAY
          Give it back.

                    TAMMY
          You gotta catch me first.

Kay lunges at the wig. Tammy moves the wig at the last
second like a matador. Kay stumbles on the coffee table.
Tammy hurries away but not before Kay grabs Tammy by the leg
tripping her.

Tammy's face bumps the coffee table. Tammy freezes, grabs
her face and starts to cry. In the jumble, the massager has
turned on to VIBRATE again.

Kay shakes her head and calmly take a sip of wine.

Tammy heads for the door with her pile of clothes, holding
her cheek.

                    KAY
          You can get out and stay out!

Kay stumbles towards her wig.

                    KAY (CONT'D)
          That girl sure is jealous of my hair.

Kay rearranges her wig and shakes her head and prepares to
get comfy on the couch again.

                    KAY (CONT'D)
          No one is gonna take care of her.

Kay lies down again. She sits up suddenly alarmed.

                    KAY (CONT'D)
          Oh Shit!

EXT. STREET

Tammy drives her Schwinn bike with its front basket filled
with clothes toward a phone booth.

                                              CUT TO:

INT. HOSPITAL ROOM - EVENING

Mitch watches TV, his leg elevated by a pulley.

Kay roars in.

              KAY
Mitch baby, Momma Kay needs your help.

              MITCH
Oh, hello Ms. Gibson.

Kay pulls the pillow out from under his back.

              KAY
It's Tammy. I think she's gone and done
something crazy.

              MITCH
Uggh.

              KAY
You are the only one who can talk some
sense into her.

Kay starts lifting him out of bed.

              MITCH
But Ms. Gibson, I can't go anywhere. My
operation is first thing in the morning.

              KAY
Sugar, I'll have you back in plenty of
time.

              MITCH
Well, where is she?

              KAY
I'm not positive, but I have an idea.
Come on now.

              MITCH
But...

Kay slings his arm over her shoulder.

INT. BUICK SKYLARK - EVENING

Kay and Mitch drive down Missouri Boulevard in Kay's well
preserved blue '79 Buick Skylark, slowing to look at various
two story motels.

> KAY
> I know she's is one of these. I just
> hope we're not too late.

> MITCH
> Too late for what?

Kay approaches the Flower Motel. A one story 50's style
drive-to-your room motel.

> KAY
> There's his Cadillac.

> MITCH
> Whose?

> KAY
> That bastard.

Kay roars up next to his car and lunges out of the car toward
the lit room. Kay peers through the curtain to see Tammy and
Chet drinking champagne kissing on the bed.

Kay bangs the door open with her shoulder but is stopped by
the chain. She presses her face through the crack a la Jack
Nicholson from "The Shining".

Mitch fumbles with his jammed door and climbs to the driver
side to get out.

> KAY (CONT'D)
> Chet! Chet!

> CHET
> What the?

Kay shoulders open the door breaking the chain lock. Mitch
hobbles up from behind.

> KAY
> Stop it! Stop it! Incest is not best!

> TAMMY
> Ewww!

> CHET
> What?!

Chet and Tammy let go of each other in shock and horror.

> KAY
> Stay away from your own damn daughter!
> This is not the game the whole family can
> play.

                    TAMMY
          Daddy?

Mitch stands in the doorway.

                    MITCH
          Your dad?

                    KAY
          I should have never gotten you messed up
          in this Triple R business.

                    CHET
          Now hold on a minute.

                    TAMMY
          Oh Mitch.

Tammy runs over to Mitch and hugs him. Mitch is bewildered.

                    CHET
          What's he doing here? And why didn't you
          tell me?!

                    KAY
               (weeping)
          You never called.

                    CHET
          Our baby?

Chet goes to comfort the nodding, crying Kay.

                    MITCH
          Wanna tell me what's going on here?

                    TAMMY
          Momma, can I?

                    KAY
          Well...if he can keep a secret.

Kay relinquishes Chet's embrace to fuddle in her purse,
brushing past a different pocket sized personal massager.
She finds her keys.

                    KAY (CONT'D)
          Take my car. Don't forget you have to
          jiggle the key in neutral.

EXT. FLOWER MOTEL -EVENING

Tammy opens the driver's side door and lets Mitch in first to
climb over to his seat. Tammy starts the car after some
trouble and over revs the engine, spewing black smoke.

INT. BUICK SKYLARK - EVENING

Tammy and Mitch drive down a residential street.

                    MITCH
          So all you girls do it. Doesn't that make
          you whores?

                    TAMMY
          It's not just for officers, silly. There
          are scholarships, cherry jobs at the
          capitol, we can get introduced to foreign
          diplomats--

                    MITCH
          Who?

                    TAMMY
          I met an Italian man one time.

Mitch rubs his face.

                    TAMMY (CONT'D)
          Sandy Richardson...she married that
          senator?

                    MITCH
          Really?

                    TAMMY
          And where do you think your uniforms come
          from?

                    MITCH
          The only thing he gets us is a keg once a
          year. Where do yours come from?

                    TAMMY
          Damn, I thought maybe something was up.

                    MITCH
          Triple R.

                    TAMMY
          You're not gonna tell no one are you?

                    MITCH
          But you have to promise me you'll stop
          right now.

                    TAMMY
          Anything for you Mitch.

Tammy pulls up to the lookout gravel pad above the river.

                    TAMMY (CONT'D)
          Here's our spot.

                    MITCH
          I remember.

Tammy slides over and starts to unbutton Mitch's jeans.

                    MITCH (CONT'D)
          Hold up there.

                    TAMMY
          What's the matter?

                    MITCH
          We gotta talk. We've been good friends
          since we were kids right?

Tammy nods.

                    MITCH (CONT'D)
          And you know I'd never want to do
          anything to hurt you, right?

                    TAMMY
          Except dating that bitch Judy.

                    MITCH
          Now...I love Judy. You and I, we're just
          really good friends.

Tammy leans google-eyed towards his crotch and throws out her
gum.

                    TAMMY
          I can do it better now, I'll show you. I
          learned to keep my teeth out of the--

Mitch stops her head.

                    TAMMY (CONT'D)
          She's not gonna be your first is she?!

                    MITCH
          I hope so.

Tammy throws a mega SCREAMING tantrum.

> TAMMY
> You were saving that for me-ee!

> MITCH
> When did I say that?

Tammy beats the steering wheel and SCREAMS. Mitch is unamused and puts his arm on her shoulder.

> TAMMY
> Don't you touch me.

Tammy goes to start the car. It won't start. She puts it in neutral. The wheel slowly creeps to the edge.

Mitch pulls up the emergency brake.

> MITCH
> Whoa Nelly.

Tammy jiggles the key and hits the steering wheel again.

> MITCH (CONT'D)
> I'll go get help.

Mitch starts out and winces in pain. Tammy jumps out.

> TAMMY
> I'll go, damn cripple. I oughtta just
> leave you here.

Tammy storms down the road towards the lights of the town.

Mitch shakes his head, turns on the radio and laughs.

> MITCH
> Triple R. Judy's gonna shit.

EXT. TOW TRUCK BUILDING -EVENING

Tammy pounds on the window. VERN, a 50ish crusty man, sleeps with his mouth open in a chair amidst messy paper and a whisky bottle.

> TAMMY
> Vern!...Vern! Wake up!

Tammy goes in the office, picks up his whisky bottle; slams it down and begins slapping his face to no response.

Tammy grabs the keys to the tow truck and walks outside.

Tammy starts the bright yellow tow truck and REVS the engine; flips on the flashing lights and SQUEALS tires away.

INT. TOW TRUCK - EVENING

Tammy grinds the gears and then drives fast while wiping her tears.

                    TAMMY
          He loves me.

INT. BUICK SKYLARK - EVENING

Mitch listens to the radio. (Suggest Eagles "Desperado") He admires the view and then hears the tow truck ROAR up from behind complete with FLASHING LIGHTS.

                    MITCH
          Cool.

Mitch sticks his head out the window and waves.

                    MITCH (CONT'D)
          Hey!

Mitch looks alarmed as he notices Tammy alone behind the wheel.

                    MITCH (CONT'D)
          Tammy, what in the hell are you doing?

Tammy sticks her head out the window.

                    TAMMY
          Say it! Say I'll be your first.

                    MITCH
          But...

Tammy revs the engine and BUMPS the car. Its braked wheels slide on the gravel. The car rests on boulders at the edge of the cliff.

                    MITCH (CONT'D)
          Are you trying to kill me?

                    TAMMY
              (hysterical)
          Just say it. Say you love me!

                    MITCH
          Why?

Tammy revs the engine and BANGS the car in to the boulders. One large boulder cascades down 200 feet.

Mitch is scared staring at the missing boulder.

                    MITCH (CONT'D)
          Tammy!

                    TAMMY
          Say it!

Tammy hits the steering wheel and BUMPS her head against the steering wheel stomping her feet. She sinks her head on the wheel.

Her foot slips to the gas and she accidentally REVS the engine sending Mitch and the Buick jettisoned over the edge.

                    TAMMY (CONT'D)
          Mitch! Oh my God! Oh my God!

CRASH!

Tammy gets out and observes the shadowy belly-upped wreckage, wheels spinning, at the river's edge 200 feet below.

                    TAMMY (CONT'D)
          My Mitch!

Tammy gets in the tow truck and roars away in shock.

EXT. TOW TRUCK OFFICE -EVENING

Tammy pulls up, lights off. She runs panicked into the office and puts the keys back on the desk. She flails down the street into the dark.

EXT. CLIFF

Mitch struggles up from the cliff. His temple badly bleeding.

INT. MARILYN'S HOUSE

Tammy hangs her head and quietly sobs.

                    MARILYN
          Jonah was on thing, but you have really
          screwed the pooch on this one.

                    TAMMY
          My Mitch.

MITCH'S POV: Headlights stream into his eyes.

INT. MARILYN'S BUICK REGAL

Marilyn sees Mitch crawling in the roadway.

                    MARILYN
          Thank you lord Jesus.

Tammy jumps out of the car to his aid.

EXT. ROAD

                    TAMMY
          Baby, you're alive.

Mitch is too exhausted and injured to speak.

                    MARILYN
          Get him in the car before the whole damn
          town sees him.

They both assist dragging Mitch inside the car.

INT. MARILYN'S BUICK REGAL

Tammy sits in the rear seat cuddling Mitch.

                    MARILYN
          We've got to get you to the hospital.

Mitch can barely speak.

                    MITCH
          You've got to stop Triple R. Stop her.

Mitch points to Marilyn. Tammy covers his mouth. Marilyn
slams on the brakes.

                    MARILYN
          Don't tell me you opened your yip trap.

                    TAMMY
          Just a little.

INT. MARILYN'S HOUSE - GUEST ROOM

Tammy and Marilyn help Mitch into a double bed.

                    MITCH
          Where am I?

                    MARILYN
          Here baby, take these. This has all been
          a dream. You're in the hospital.

Marilyn shakes out two pills, and then shakes out two more.
She helps administer them to him with water. She pats his
forehead, pushing his head down on the pillow. She points
Tammy to the other room.

INT. LIVING ROOM

               MARILYN
      Maybe I can get the good doctor to
      scramble his brain or something. But if
      not, I'm going to have to take care of
      him myself.

               TAMMY
      You wouldn't.

               MARILYN
      Then you best be doing what I say from
      here on out.

Tammy nods and looks towards Mitch's room.

INT. CHET'S OFFICE - EVENING

Chet speaks on the phone.

               CHET
      You haven't delivered on your end of the
      bargain.

INT. MARILYN'S BEDROOM

               MARILYN
      We've had a few complications.

INTERCUT AS NEEDED

               CHET
      You just let me know when you want out,
      cause there's a line out the Capitol
      building waiting for your job.

               MARILYN
      Well. Does she have to be awake for it?

Chet thinks about it.

               CHET
      I suppose not...

INT. HOSPITAL ROOM

Judy waits at the empty bed holding a large BOUQUET of
FLOWERS. A nurse enters.

                              JUDY
              Where'd they move him?

                              NURSE
              Doc Gardner said he's in intensive care
              and not to be disturbed. Come back
              tomorrow.

                              JUDY
              Intensive care?

Judy is puzzled, disappointed and watches the nurse leave.
She walks into the hallway.

INT. HOSPITAL HALLWAY

Judy observes the PLACARD and follows the arrow toward
INTENSIVE CARE.

INT. ENTRANCE - INTENSIVE CARE

Judy pokes open the door. She notices an OLD MAN on a
respirator and FOUR EMPTY BEDS.

                              MARILYN (O.S.)
              There you are.

Judy spins around.

                              MARILYN (CONT'D)
              I've been looking all over for you,
              Congratulations!

Judy looks back at the ICU door. Marilyn turns her away.

                              MARILYN (CONT'D)
              We're having a little celebration over at
              my house. You've been selected as an
              officer!

Marilyn takes her by the shoulders, almost pushing her out
the door.

INT. MARILYN'S HOUSE

Marilyn takes Judy's BOUQUET and puts it in a large vase on
her shiny wooden banquet.

                              JUDY
              Where is everyone?

                              MARILYN
              Guess we're the first ones here.

Judy is suspicious.

Marilyn goes to the kitchen.

INT. KITCHEN

Marilyn retrieves a bottle of CHAMPAGNE from the fridge. She
pops open a prescription BOTTLE and opens 4 capsules into one
of the glasses.

Mitch MOANS in the background.

                    JUDY
          What's that?

Marilyn mimics the sound.

                    MARILYN
          (singing a la "Star is Born")
          "One, ageless endeavor"

Marilyn enters with two glasses of champagne.

INT. LIVING ROOM

                    MARILYN
          I like to sing when I'm happy.

Judy looks out the window at Chet's ELDORADO and then back at
Marilyn's scary fake smile.

INT. GUEST BEDROOM

Chet forces another pill down Mitch's throat.

INT. LIVING ROOM

Marilyn hands Judy the tainted glass and beelines to the
stereo, turning it on a little too loud.

                    MARILYN
          Bottom's up!

Judy looks at her glass and then Marilyn's. Something is not
right. She stares into Marilyn's suspicious eyes.

                    MARILYN (CONT'D)
          Well, what you waiting for? There's
          plenty more where that come from.

Marilyn downs hers and nervously heads to the kitchen.

INT. KITCHEN

Marilyn refills her glass and returns with the bottle.
Judy's glass is empty.

                    MARILYN
          Atta girl.

Marilyn refills Judy's glass.

                    JUDY
          Thanks.

                    MARILYN
          Lie down, I mean sit down and make
          yourself comfortable.

Marilyn motions her to the chaise lounge. Judy complies and
gets comfortable on the chaise.

                    MARILYN (CONT'D)
          I'll go call the girls and see what's
          taking them.

Marilyn enters the bedroom.

INT. GUEST BEDROOM

Chet warms his hands together in anticipation. Mitch is
passed out in the background.

                    MARILYN
          That was a close one.

Marilyn looks at Mitch.

                    CHET
          Is she ready?

                    MARILYN
          Give it time boy.

Chet jumps up and down.

                    MARILYN (CONT'D)
          And don't be ramming it in there like a
          butter churner or she'll know something's
          up tomorrow.

                    CHET
          Oh, all right.

Marilyn motions for him to wait and exits.

INT. LVIING ROOM

Judy is passed out on the chaise. Marilyn walks over to her
and caresses her hair. She leans in.

                    MARILYN
          Judy?

Marilyn lightly slaps her face. Judy is motionless.

Marilyn walks back to the bedroom, opens the door and motions
for Chet to come out.

                    MARILYN (CONT'D)
          No more than your normal three minutes.

                    CHET
          Hot dog!

Chet takes off his shirt, but leaves his wife-beater t-shirt
on. He walks in front of Judy and spreads her limp legs. He
pulls down his pants to reveal his fat bottom wrapped by a G-
String. He pulls down the G-String.

The bouquet of FLOWERS on the banquet is limp and drooping.

CLOSE UP: Judy's face. Judy appears to be squinting through
her closed eyes.

Judy's eyes pop open.

She grabs what must be his penis and twists it hard enough to
break it off.

Chet reels backward in pain SCREAMING.

Marilyn comes to his rescue. Judy jumps up and flips Marilyn
on the floor, knocking the wind out of her.

Judy hears the MOAN and runs to the bedroom.

INT. BEDROOM

Judy jerks open the door.

                    JUDY
          Mitch.

Mitch, although delirious, recognizes Judy and is excited to
see her.

                    MITCH
          Judy.

She runs to him and hugs him.

                    MITCH (CONT'D)
          Triple R. Don't do it.

Mitch is listless. Judy nods.

                    MARILYN (O.S.)
          Hold it right there.

Marilyn stands in the doorway holding a small gun. Chet
waddles up behind her with his pants still around his ankles,
whimpering.

                    CHET
          I think she broke it.

                    MARILYN
          Stand back.

                    CHET
          You're not gonna kill them?

                    MARILYN
          Thanks to your new "daughter", there's no
          choice. And I just got that new
          bedspread at Penneys.

Marilyn looks down at Chet's crotch. Judy seizes the
opportunity and throws an old fashioned ALARM CLOCK resting
on the bedstand at Marilyn, knocking the gun out of her hand.

Marilyn pushes Chet out of the way. His restricted legs
force him to kick the gun even further away into the kitchen.

Judy and Marilyn both scramble for the gun. It is a fight to
the death, a struggle of might.

                    CHET
          We can all work this out.

Judy now sits on top of Marilyn near the kitchen door. They
both have a hand on the GUN. Marilyn tries to point the gun
at Judy.

Just then, the KITCHEN DOOR jerks open. Slamming Marilyn in
the head and knocking her unconscious.

                    TAMMY
          Mitch?

Tammy looks down, holding a bucket of KENTUCKY FRIED CHICKEN.

                    TAMMY (CONT'D)
          Oh Shit. I thought you and Chet were
          supposed to...

Tammy looks behind them to see Chet whimpering down at his
crotch.

                    CHET
          It's gone.

                    TAMMY
          I better leave now.

Tammy drops the bucket and runs out the back door.

Judy drags Marilyn's body, feet first, to the kitchen closet
and locks it.

Judy runs by Chet nursing his proboscis and kicks him hard in
the back, sending him sprawling forward.

She runs to Mitch's room. He is still in delirium. She can't
leave him.

                    JUDY
          Stay here.

Judy kisses him, walks to the door, locks it from the inside
and closes it.

EXT. JUDY'S HOUSE

A paper boy slams down the Jefferson City NEWS TRIBUNE on the
front steps.

It reads: TOP LEGISLATOR CAUGHT IN TEEN SEX SCANDAL. More
arrests expected.

SUPER: 2 MONTHS LATER

INT. HIGH SCHOOL HALLWAY

Judy walks with her head held high through the crowded
hallway. She is the premier celebrity. Everyone from the
geeks to the goddesses say hello. Scott walks by with two
junior babes, one on each arm, and gives her a nod. Judy
shakes her head. Lori approaches her.

                    LORI
          Good morning Miss President.

                    JUDY
          Good morning Miss Secretary.

                    LORI
          You can't miss this one tonight.

                    JUDY
          I'll be there.

Mitch hobbles up on crutches, wearing a backpack. They kiss
a kiss of true love. Lori blushes.

INT. JAIL WAITING ROOM -AFTERNOON

Kay wears her bouffant wig with her medallion. She sits
across from Tammy dressed in her jail house blues looking
disheveled.

                    KAY
          Baby, I brought you some of these.

Kay produces some Jenny Craig meals.

                    KAY (CONT'D)
          I figured since I was already eating
          them, I could add them to my product
          line. I've lost four pounds.

                    TAMMY
          Momma, there's no microwave here for me.

Tammy pushes them back.

                    KAY
          Baby, cheer up. 5 months versus their 10
          years ain't squat.

                    TAMMY
          Easy for you to say.

A large scary woman approaches Tammy from behind and fiddles
with Tammy's hair.

                    SCARY WOMAN
               (gruff)
          Who's she.

                    TAMMY
          Would you get your damn hands off me!

Tammy twists scary woman's fingers but scary woman puts her
other hand on Tammy's shoulder. Kay gets riled.

                    KAY
          I am her mother.

Kay stands and brushes scary woman's other hand from Tammy.

Scary woman knocks off Kay's wig with her free hand. Kay goes crazy and lunges at scary woman. Tammy buries her face in her hands.

INT. 57 CHEVY TRUCK

Scott drives Mitch's truck. Mitch sits in the middle with Judy in the passenger seat. The truck stops. Judy gets out.

> JUDY
> Ok Mario, come back in an hour.

Scott revs the engine and peels away.

EXT. STREET

Judy shakes her head and walks into a ranch style home.

INT. LIVING ROOM

The Triple R girls are giddy and excited that Judy is in their presence.

> JUDY
> Ok girls. This meeting will now come to
> order.

Carolyn and Becky continue talking. Without being asked, they stop talking and submit their fines with a smile to the TRIPLE R PIGGY BANK.

Judy stops them by putting her hand over the slot. They smile appreciatively.

> JUDY (CONT'D)
> In fact. Free Pizza.

Judy turns the pig over and removes the black rubber stopper. She begins to shake the pig. Something blocks the hole. She reaches her index finger inside and pulls out her missing white UNDERWEAR. Hundreds of COINS and the seam RIPPER clank on the coffee table.

Judy isn't surprised.

> JUDY (CONT'D)
> I missed these.

Judy stuff her underwear in her jeans. She scoops the coins together in a pile.

> JUDY (CONT'D)
> This meeting will now come to order.

The group is silent with admiration.

>   JUDY (CONT'D)
>   As your new president. I would like to
>   make a few new rules.

The group looks on with anticipation.

>   JUDY (CONT'D)
>   I would like to make a motion to close
>   Triple R forever.

The girls are stunned and speechless. Lori gives her a hug.

>   CAROLYN
>   But Judy. You're it. Now you can do
>   whatever you want to do.

>   JUDY
>   And this is what I want to do.

Judy nods to Lori. Lori is filled with joy.

>   JUDY (CONT'D)
>   All those in favor?

>   LORI
>   I!

>   BECKY
>   I!

And the rest of the group follows suit almost simultaneously,
ending with Carolyn who finally feels free.

Judy takes an armful of coins and throws them in to the air
where they FREEZE.

>   FADE OUT: